The Doomsday Club

Alex Damien

GLENNEYRE PRESS
LOS ANGELES, CA

Printed in the United States of America.

Published by Glenneyre Press, LLC.
Los Angeles, CA
http://www.glenneyrepress.com
Email: info@glenneyrepress.com

First Edition

ISBN 0-9768040-0-x

This is a work of fiction. Any similarity of characters or events to real
persons or actual events is coincidental.

*To Mr. and Mrs. America
and all the ships at sea...*

ONE

Hale doesn't really seem to notice your life has headlonged into a massive clusterfuck of sorts. Not that you ever really expect him to but in your sometimes incredibly naive way of thinking, you've been hoping he'll mention that you haven't showered, shaved, gone outside in days, or eaten much more than Cheetos from the rusted-out, hunk of junk vending machine down the hall. For Christ's sake, the least he could do is mention the haircut you've given yourself. Though, you suppose if it was your roommate turning into a dirty, reeking, Cheeto-eating poster boy for mental patient hairstyles, you'd probably do your best to say nothing either. Truly, the funniest thing about this is that if he would just crack open one of his Psych textbooks long enough, he might even recognize this as a complete cry for help on your part.

It's around the fourth or fifth day that he finally says something about it.

"I used to call her Mitten because she smothered you and gave you absolutely no distinctive form."

You glare daggers into his soul as he shakes his head.

"Thank you, drive through," you respond.

At this point Hale picks up the framed photo on your desk, the one you've been unable to look away from since falling into this funk—a snap of Jackie and you in better times, and frisbees it through the open window.

You yelp as if he had carved out your spleen with a wooden spoon, knowing if you weren't feeling so damned helpless you might sock him in the eye. Instead, you sit and stare at the empty space the photo of the woman you once loved had, until just now, occupied. To Hale's credit, at least he doesn't remind you that this is the second time this month you've been kicked to the curb.

Last year, Coach Riggs moved you from the outfield to starting shortstop. A lot of your teammates had hopes for getting to the bigs after graduation but you knew you'd never have the chops to go to the show so you were just happy not to ride pine. As a complete surprise to no one, you had a very lackluster season. You didn't quite suck but you didn't really shine either—except once.

In your inimitable way you blamed your sorry-ass excuse of an on-base percentage on the lack of a good bat. Everybody thought it was a steaming load, but in your gut you truly believed it. Jackie had gotten so sick of hearing about it that right before the third to last game of the season she bought you a brand new aluminum Louisville Slugger and damn if it didn't look like something King Arthur could have pulled from a stone to slay a dragon with. On the spot, you dubbed it Excalibur. Jackie threw her arms around you, kissed you and said the words that put the ping back into your swing:

"Get thee a hit and thou mayest bed a lusty wench this evening."

You went three for four that afternoon, including the triple that scored the game-winning run. You even homered in each of the last two games of the season. That damn bat made all the difference in your swing and your confidence and you treated it like some sort of holy relic by mounting it on a rack on the wall above your bed. This year, though, your mind is elsewhere and you field like someone punched a hole in your glove. At the plate you can't see the ball to save your life. When Coach Riggs pulls you aside to say he's making room for someone else on the roster until you get your head on straight, you pack your stuff and leave without saying a single word.

When Hale comes back twenty minutes later, having replaced the shattered frame with something cheap from the market down the street, you snatch it from him with both hands. Your heart still sinks. Jackie a.k.a. "Mitten" had been your steady girl for most of the last twenty-six months, two weeks and three days and the fact that she'd ejected you from her life with all of the fanfare usually reserved for tossing a cigarette butt from a car window was not exactly a state secret around here anymore. Nor was the fact that she had done so because you had become one unbearably morose son of a bitch.

Made you wonder how come you were always the last to know. Never before it happens but boy if a moment of horrifying enlightenment didn't strike you between the eyes just as the words were about to spill out of her mouth. You have this crazy theory. You think your balls know and they crawl right up into your belly. They do a duck and cover and all of sudden you sense them pushing up against your gut and you know that it's all turned into a big nine-ways-to-Sunday pooch-screw. It just beat the hell out of you how they got to be so damn smart in the first place.

And that's when Hale sighs, reaches into his dresser drawer and does what he thinks would be best. He packs a very, very large bong hit for the two of you.

"A friend with weed..." he offers.

"Is a friend indeed," you shoot back. Hale grins at you and today more than ever with that poker-straight hair of his he has that Messiah look that some dudes just have. Jesus with a joint, that is. You often think your little saying is kind of stupid but you do it because it's one of those things that started four years ago and sort of stuck because tradition in a college dorm is saving twenty cases of empties so you can build a beer-can pyramid in the back of your room.

"Dude, you want more of this?" Hale passes the joint to you. "I think I've had more hits than the Rolling Stones."

You smoke for a good hour during which time you're joined by Nikko Desic—this real smart, round-shouldered, kind of pimply kid with an underdeveloped face that looks like it could have used more womb time, and your buddy Fuckin' Dan, a skinny guy who can barely put three syllables together without dropping the F-bomb like some kind of redneck *Enola Gay*. These are your best friends. In private, Hale often half-jokes about someday publishing a paper declaring Dan's profane condition as some sort of speech impediment or something. Right now you could care less.

At this moment, the only thing you know is that for the first time in almost a week you feel nearly human again. Somewhere just north of shit-fire awful and south of fine. You're in metamorphosis from homeless-looking, manic depressive dipshit into giggly, smiley, stoned guy and you feel your pain melt away.

"Who fuckin' wears Polo shirts anymore?" Dan points a finger at the little man riding the embroidered horse on Nikko's chest.

"I got it," Hale says. "I'm gonna get some of those from Hong Kong, but instead of an Equestrian, I'll have some Chinese convict laborers sew a guy in a wheelchair on the chest and I'll call them *Polio* shirts. I'm serious, I could make a million bucks."

To everyone's annoyance, you start to find every goddamned thing funny. You laugh like hell at the monster zit on Nikko's forehead, at a dirty cartoon titled *Bi-curious George* that Hale shows you, at your self-inflicted hair wound and more than anything else, you laugh at the bright orange Cheeto stains that look like they'll need to be sandblasted off your fingers. Suddenly you're engrossed, knowing there's no way whatever makes those damn things that godawful color could be anything other than exceedingly detrimental to your health. Your mind races to thoughts of wearing gloves to the dinner table when you go home so the Units don't ask why your hands sport a lovely shade of dayglow toxic-shock monkey piss. Maybe, you think, if it comes down to that you'll buy a pair of oven mitts so you can give your stepdad the finger whenever you feel like it, which incidentally is getting to be quite a lot when you're home.

In a way, you know the city is doing this to you. You're a suburban boy with soft hands. *Maybe I don't belong here*, you wonder. And as you feel a kind of bubbling euphoric moment of clarity, you stop laughing because of the wave of paranoia that hits you like a sucker punch.

Ten minutes ago you had gotten up to take a leak and when you came back, you were in such a rush to toke up, you forgot to put the towel back under the crack in the door to keep the smoke from leaking out into the hall. This year you couldn't even smoke cigs in this building, let alone doobage, and Hale was very adamant about the whole towel deal. Last year you watched as he got busted more times than James Brown at a wife-beating convention. So many times, in fact, the school threatened to boot his ass out entirely. His father, the ex-stuntman turned porn producer, a stocky fucker who went by the nickname of *Bullet*, got so pissed that he left the set of *Anal Fisted Bitches With Badges 3* to come here and give Hale an earful that you could hear from your old room on the other side of the floor. The old man told him, in no uncertain terms, that if Hale got himself punted from yet another school he'd get his ass beaten *Brooklyn style*, whatever the hell that meant. So, like any good boy Hale swore he'd straighten up and fly right and that he'd stop smoking pot, a promise he kept for nearly six whole hours after his dad got in the Seven-series and pedaled his deluded old self back to his house in Topanga Canyon and the twenty-year old trophy wife with giant pillowy tits.

This year, Hale lives with you. You get along well but you feel fairly certain it's because you're here on scholarship and he wants his dad to think he's stopped hanging out with his burner friends. His parents buy into it—hook, line and stinker. They love you. You're on the cusp of making something of your life. Little do they know your grades are sinking, your habit is getting as bad as his lately and the two of you account for most of the narf smoked on this floor. You just have the common sense to confine most of your shaking and baking to that little park on Mulholland where you and Jackie used to go sit and watch the lights of Hollywood twinkle like a tray of jewels after a good backseat romp.

And as you toke it up with your pals in your room with what is probably half the floor getting ripped on the second-hand smoke leaking out from the crack under the door, you look around and see nobody else has noticed the missing towel. You tell yourself if you can just put the damn thing back where it belongs, it's no harm, no foul, no big deal. You reach down into your crotch to check, and to your relief the boys are where they belong. Rock on, brother. Rock on.

As soon as Hale hits off the bong, you reach over to grab the towel and immediately see the thin shaft of light from underneath the door broken by the tree-trunk shadows of a large pair of combat boots on the other side. And even before the heavy knock on the door comes you know exactly that it's the last person on this whole spinning rock that you want to see right now.

Richard "Bo" Boyd, the Resident Assistant on your floor, is without a single iota of doubt, the epitome of low-voltage social reject Marine ROTC attracts on this campus. About guys like Bo, Hale has a theory he's dubbed the *teenie weenie syndrome*. Men with little dicks grow up over-aggressively trying to measure up against other males. Pity is that even though women can see right through this gross overcompensation, they get drawn to this type of mate because of how easily they can control him by letting him believe he's just as big as anyone else. The often overlooked and sad part of the whole damn thing is that if the woman remains unsatisfied sexually, she may decide to hunt down an extracurricular larger organ. Thus threatening her mate's newly found status of manhood and he in turn vents his aggressions on her. Deep down, you often think if Hale would ever get around to actually writing his thesis it would be about reducing domestic violence by making men less angry at their own dicks.

The school year didn't start with Bo or else you would have transferred to the newly co-ed girls' college down the street. In the Fall, when you moved in to find Becky Aldredge as the R.A.—kind of cute, kind of a chub-chub and a little bit granola around the edges—you all figured you had it made in the shade. You figured a little fiirting with the Beckster would ensure never getting busted for squat.

Well, if you had known that any right-minded man trying to wink at a feminist lesbian was apt to get his dick kicked in the dirt, you would have nixed the idea from the get go. Turned out the Beckster thought the four of you were goofing on her and got her panties all knotted in a bunch. Next thing you know, Hale was getting busted regularly and the simple easygoing life you'd worked so hard to attain had gone the way of the hot comb.

Two weeks before Christmas break and you were on the prowl at this Omega Chi party in Westwood and lo and behold, there was Becky's girlfriend hanging out looking like she was hoping someone would go and talk her up. Now, unlike the Beckster, this chick was borderline hot—nice frame and a slow gap-toothed smile on the marginal side of sexy. Nothing to break your arm writing home about but in the general all-around, not too shabby and there wasn't a straight man in attendance who hadn't done much worse at one time or another. You figured all the drunken frat jerks would be crawling all over her, right? Well, all the Omega Chis knew she batted the other side of the plate and everyone there was trying their best to score at least one last party lay before break. So, as a result, the Beckster's girl was flying solo.

You pooled your cash and came up with close to a hundred bucks and Nikko tossed it to one of his buds from the basketball team to go over and start flirting with her. Hale whipped out a camera phone and after an hour of googly eyes and a few more jello shots you became the proud owners of a snapshot of Becky's honey pie jamming her tongue down the throat of one of the biggest black dudes you'd ever seen in your life.

You end up in such a rush to get back to your room to e-mail it to the Wicked Bitch of the West Wing that you actually miss the best part of the whole damn evening. It turned out that Nikko's buddy, Wallace, took Becky's girlfriend back to the jock dorm and gave her the time until the wee hours of the morning.

Becky found the picture in her e-mail the next day and went positively apeshit. They broke up, Beckster swallowed a handful of OxyContin, and after a long night of puking her guts out in the infirmary she went back home to Idaho and to the best of anyone's knowledge. No one had seen hide nor hairy leg of her since. "It just goes to show you," Hale said as her taxi pulled away. "Pussy makes you crazy no matter who you are."

As the pounding on your door continues, Dan whispers, "Oh shit, it's Major fuckin' Dick!" and Hale bursts out giggling, blowing a mouthful of smoke right in your face. The laughter is completely contagious because Nikko and Dan can't help giggling like drunken ten-year old girls. Not you though. What you get is a major case of the jumpies that old Bo is going to hand you some noise about your orange-stained fingers or your shitty homemade haircut. You realize then, pot does some very weird stuff to you sometimes.

"I said, open this goddammed door right now! I'm going to write up the whole bunch of you misfit motherfuckers!"

Hearing the chuckling through the door was pissing Bo off even more because he starts barking it now, just like the way they teach when you're up to your ass in a river full of piranhas and God-knows-what and you have to give an order to all the other automatons in the platoon. In a whisper, Hale dares somebody to ask through the door if *Semper Fi* comes from ancient Latin for *I am a fucking robot.*

But you're still gaping at the shadows of Bo's shoes under the crack in the door when Hale calls your name, waking you out of your paranoid trance. You are completely sober again. That sinking feeling of depression has come back like a bad check.

"Scott, open the door," Hale says again.

You look over at him while Nikko just shrugs his shoulders back in a calm way that makes you think if you were to take his pulse right then and there it would barely break sixty.

Yours on the other hand beats like a dance club kick drum and you feel it in your temples. You reach over and turn the knob and the door slams open, crashing against the wall and startling all of you. Bo stands there for a second, puts his hands on his hips and does his best General Patton tight-ass walk into the room.

And this is the point where Hale unfortunately decides to show off his finely honed sarcasm.

"Can I help you?" he asks, doing his best impression of someone who never gave a shit about anything even remotely authoritarian.

Bo squints at him the way you'd look at a dog turd stuck to the bottom of your shoe. Then, making absolutely sure that he has eye contact with all of you, he blurts: "You little rat-fucks are big-time busted."

Busted.

The word hangs in the air like a stale odor and you can tell Bo is enjoying this far too much and you absolutely begin to hate his stupid jarhead guts for it. Right then, you get this feeling deep down inside that nothing good can possibly come out of all of this.

Your balls know.

Duck and cover.

"Now, I don't know what kind of bullshit Little Miss Muffdive let you jerks get away with but let me be the first to inform you that it won't be tolerated any longer. You little dopers make me sick. I'm not about to let this go down on my watch, especially by little stoner faggots like you!"

He works his way up to a cadence and you suddenly become aware of the need to go pee again. Major Dick looks at you with those crazy eyes of his and you feel your boys decide to go hibernate for the winter.

"Congratulations," he growls at you. "It looks like you'll end up with this whole room to yourself after they kick your loser roommate out of school."

You steal a glance at Hale but he just keeps his poker face.

"That is, if they let you keep your scholarship." Bo knows he has your full and undivided attention.

"Tell you what. I'm even going to confiscate your stash so you little drug addicts won't be lighting up until after they boot all of your asses out," he adds, and that becomes enough to loosen up Nikko's tongue.

"Hey man, you can't do that!"

"Shut your suck, fucknut. Maybe you haven't noticed it from your little drug-induced haze over there but there isn't a soul on this floor right now but you scumbags and me. That means I could throw all of you down the fucking elevator shaft and say it was a weirdo tragic accident or some little stoner faggot suicide pact. Since I'm in a good mood, I'm just going to take your precious little dope down to the can myself and before I flush it, I'm going to drop my pants and take a great big crap all over it."

You all flinch as Bo's fleshy paw shoots out to grab your weed from the desk behind Nikko's head.

"Just what I thought, just a bunch of little pussy-boys," he says, crunching the rolled up baggie in his fist like a Sioux warrior taking a cowboy's scalp.

As he turns on his heels and walks out, your hope that he makes it halfway to Neptune before anyone says anything gets shattered by Dan.

"Fuckin' dick," your buddy mutters underneath his breath.

As Bo stops in his tracks, you swallow hard. "What did you say?" Bo barks as he snaps around on his heels.

Silence.

Bo stands there, milking it to the point of sheer agony.

"What'd you say, fuckstain?" Bo's nostrils flare and it flashes into your head that he has at least three inches and no less than sixty pounds over any of you. Wiping up a room full of pot-smoking smartasses is probably stepping into wet dream territory for him.

Dan stands up, and you want to punch him in the mouth for getting you all in way deeper shit than you were in already.

He looks Bo square in the eye. "I was fuckin' wondering. If your parents got a divorce, would they still be considered cousins?"

You expect instant Hiroshima, but what Bo does scares you even more. He snorts, takes one step into your room and shuts the door behind him. Without a word he makes it very clear how this is going to be a very private ass-kicking for all of you.

"It's gonna get busier than a pair of jumper cables at a Puerto Rican wedding in here." Bo grunts, puts his hand on Nikko's face and shoves him into your dresser, knocking over the newly re-framed picture of you and Jackie taken at the beach last summer. Helplessly, you watch as Jackie and you hit the floor and as the glass breaks, you suddenly want so badly to be on that beach with her, drinking margaritas and making love in the chest high water instead of facing the ugly prospect of a mouth full of broken chiclets.

You don't know how long you space out but when you turn around, Bo has Dan in a choke hold. Dan's face starts to turn purple and Hale tries to pry Bo's thick arms away with one hand while pushing his face back with the other. When you see Bo grinning like the Cheshire Cat after a blowjob, something inside you finally rages like a furnace.

"Do something!" Hale turns to you. The sudden blast of adrenaline feels like heroin jacking through your veins. A dry lump the size of Mexico fills your throat.

"Fucking *do* something!" Hale screams again and in one flash you know how to make it all go away. You know how to take control of the situation, make the yelling subside and bring back the calming sense of silence you now miss so much.

Your eyes dart to the relic mounted over your bed. Without a sound you feel the world stop turning as your fingers wrap around its handle.

You take a breath. You close your eyes.

And in one split-second you swing Excalibur again and change all of your lives forever.

2

After hearing the ping of the aluminum Louisville Slugger against Bo's skull, there is no mistaking that this one is over the fence and headed for the cheap seats. He gurgles and instantly goes limp, letting go of Dan and falling to the floor like a bag of hammers.

You stand there just looking at each other for what seems like the longest time. Dan, who always had a gift for stating the obvious, says it first though:

"Jesus fuckin' Christ, Dude! You just killed Major Dick!"

Bo is lying on the floor of your dorm room deader than dogshit and all eyes are on you. Well, no doubt about it, you killed him alright. Lights out. Game over. Ladies and gentlemen, goodnight. Elvis has left the fucking planet.

Strangely enough, you are calm though, mostly because it hasn't, no pun intended, really hit you yet what had just happened until Dan starts getting the shakes and tries to puke into the trashcan under your desk. At that moment you want to be able to shake and puke but to tell you the truth you know that you won't because you are feeling too, well, high. Not off of the Mexican Brown that Bo still has in the baggie clutched tightly in his cold dead fingers but off of the adrenaline jacking through your veins. You felt a rush like this the first time you homered in a college game; you felt one the time you tried skydiving last summer; and you think you got a rush off of the first time you ever kissed Jackie, but nothing compared to the buzz you are on now. Adrenaline is like heroin for your soul, a straight mainline into your id. You know that you aren't going to be sick; you know that you aren't going to panic. You know, because in some weird way you are feeling better at that moment than you have ever felt in your whole damn life.

What brings you hurtling back into the present, however, is your agonizingly full bladder now screaming at you to go relieve yourself. Holding it back is like trying to stop a locomotive with nothing more than a spongecake. You are moments away from pissing in your pants and if there ever was a time you could have gotten away with it in front of your friends, this was it. Instead, you glance over at Hale and hand him the bat.

"I really have to whiz," you tell him and before he can say anything you are halfway down the hall to the can. It is probably the very last thing he expected you to say at that moment next to *I'm going to Disneyland.*

The bathroom is empty and you take the first urinal and uncork old faithful. It always seems to occur to you during those moments when your bladder feels as if it might just burst like an overripe melon that a good piss is nearly as satisfying as good sex or a great sneeze. You close your eyes.

What happened in your room seems like something from

another world entirely—another time and another place. It was like you just watched it on TV, not like something that really ever happened, at least not to you. Your head is throbbing viciously and your throat is dry and sticky. You are crashing hard from your newfound high already. Cheap shit that adrenaline, no wonder people shoot skag instead.

You go to the sink to splash some water on your face. In the mirror the visage looking back at you vaguely resembles Scott Lorlon, B average student and second-rate ballplayer.

"Second rate my ass," you tell yourself. "That one would have been out of Commiskey, would have cleared the Big Green Monster in Fenway on its way to smashing into the Citgo sign in Kenmore Square. Barry Bonds can suck my motherfucking dick."

Part of you wants to laugh but instead all you can do is picture Bo lying on the floor of your room. He is stone dead and you should be sitting in Fluid Dynamics instead of thinking you are going to end up in jail. Do not pass Go, kiss your ride, your future and your anal virginity goodbye. Your balls are no longer hibernating, they have skipped town. Vaya con fucking Dios. This past week has been the shit week to end all shit weeks. First Jackie leaves and now Bo. Ladies and gentlemen, meet the great Fuck-upski and for your next trick you're going to blow lunch. It's now your turn to be sick.

You puke in the sink.

When you get back, Dan is sitting on your bed, his purple face now red and flushed and you can see he's been crying. You want to say something to him but you're drawing a big donut. There is probably a reason why there wasn't a Hallmark card for someone whose attacker you've just baseball batted into eternity.

"We're going to jail," Nikko says, grabbing your sleeve.

"Jail?" Dan jumps in between sobs. "Fuck jail, my dad is going to kick my fuckin' ass!"

Hale is getting agitated because this same conversation has been going on since you left to piss out a river. You are all on the verge of panic. Understandably so. "Look, I said nobody's going to jail." He looks over at you to back him up on this one. "We just have to think, dammit."

Like a complete idiot, all you can do is nod your head in agreement. You look slike some freaking bobblehead doll. Back in the room for sixty seconds and you are already batting oh-for-two as far as having the right thing to say to anybody.

Bo is still lying there exactly where he fell since nobody dared touch him. More than anything, you want to have that dead sack of shit out of this room but it is obvious you aren't going to be able to leave him by the door like a case of empties. Hale is right, Nikko is right and Dan is right—unless someone thought of something quickly, your lives are about to shit the bed in ways you can barely begin to understand.

As a kid, the worst trouble you'd ever been in was the time you put a baseball on a golf tee in your backyard one summer and 3-ironed it dead-smack right into the neighbor's bedroom window. Nobody got hurt but it cost seventy bucks to fix and your stepdad tanned your hide but good. For the rest of that summer and all of the next you had to cut the neighbor's lawn once a week to pay for it. Man, were you pissed. Not at your stepdad or the neighbor but at your own stupid self for getting into this mess in the first place. The most important thing you learned from the whole thing was the value of not getting caught. The value of not leaving behind a baseball with your name written all over it like a complete and utter bonehead.

"Hey man, it was self defense."

Hale is working the room to no avail. It's completely limp but at least he is making the effort. Roll that rock up the hill, Sisyphus. Keep it coming. Nikko, however, isn't convinced.

"Nobody's going to believe that. There's four of us and one of him. We're going to jail," he says morosely. He is almost crying, too. This is getting worse by the second. You can't help but lose your cool and yell at him.

"Shut up! Nobody's going anywhere until we figure this out!"

Getting up and catching his breath, Dan stands over the lifeless Major Dick still sprawled on the floor. Other than a very thin trickle of blood slowly leaking out of his nose and mouth you'd think he was just lying there sound asleep. Except for the open and glassy eyes, that is.

"Fuckin' piece of shit was getting a boner trying to kill me!" Dan screams at the body. "I could feel it digging into my back."

The mere thought of this makes you wince and you look over at Hale. He is feeling queasy about it and you can see he is thinking the same thing as you are. Isn't it bad enough to have someone trying to strangle you without your last living thought on this planet be of his erection jamming into your back? Just the thought of it gives you the willies.

Dan brings his leg back and kicks Major Dick in the shoulder hard enough to spray more droplets of blood out of Bo's nose onto the floor. The motion, the movement—it reminds you of a slow motion film you saw in fluid dynamics last semester. You wonder if they are watching that in class right now.

"Fuck you, you stupid, dead, dumb, jarhead, asshole!" Dan yells at him again.

You feel your stomach nearly turn over, absolutely sure you'll vomit if he decides to do his Beckham impression on Bo again

"My dad is going to kill me too," Nikko sobbed.

"SHUT THE FUCK UP!" You all yell at him.

Hale points to the dead body on the floor. "I never realized this before, Nikko, but you and Bo could almost pass for brothers."

Christ, he's kind of right. Maybe more like a pathetically anemic second cousin than a brother, but there is a passing resemblance. You had never noticed it either until now. Hale is doing his best to try and lighten the mood with a little gallows humor. Nikko is still on the verge of tears and, as you expect, doesn't appreciate it one tiny bit.

"Fuck you!" He busts into another sob. "Fuck all of you!"

This is no time to panic. Instead of coming up with any thoughts as to how you are going to get your ass out of this, all you are thinking over and over is that this is absolutely the wrong time for hysterics. A nice toke right now would kickstart the old noggin. Put the ping back into your swing.

"I'm going to light up," you say.

Conversation stops dead as everybody looks at you. Their eyes all saying it's definitely the thing to do. It's time for a little Chilly Willy before you start jumping out of your skin. You had all been thinking about it, you are just the first one to say anything.

"Good idea," Hale says to you. "But first we have to play a little hide the Dick."

He was right. First thing was get Bo out of sight. The fact that nobody else had come by this whole time was a small miracle unto itself. Yours is one of those rooms that just sort of became a hangout pad for everyone you knew. The nights you'd usually go off and study in the library Hale would be like Hef, entertaining at the crib. The thought of someday coming back to the room and finding him in a smoking jacket with an ascot and a joint used to crack you up to no end.

There is really only one place that a six-foot-four, two-hundred and thirty pound Marine is going to fit in this room and that is the closet. Hale has never believed in hanging stuff up so his junk is all piled at the bottom as is almost all of your baseball gear. But it was either that or you just prop old Bo up at your desk with a pair of shades on his face. You try not to panic at the thought that he might not fit in there.

It takes all four of you to pick him up off of the floor and the first thing you notice is that Bo stinks of sweat and Polo cologne. You start thinking you'll end up with that smell on your hands and, like the toxic-shock-monkeypiss-orange Cheeto stains, you'll never be able to wash it off. You almost drop him but then figure the sooner you get him hidden, the sooner you're going to toke and the sooner you're going to feel like you're not going to barf anymore. Nikko is white as a sheet and if he is going to be the man and hang in there then you certainly aren't going to be a puss about it. You certainly don't look but you wonder if Bo still has the hard-on that Dan said he felt in his back. The closest any of you had ever come to a dead person before was seeing one in a movie or on TV and here you are with your hands under the armpit of a corpse trying not to think about getting its aftershave on you. Dear fucking diary...

"Back in the closet where you belong," Dan says, wiping his hands off onto his jeans and shutting the door.

"Well, that sucked." Now it was your turn to state the obvious. Nikko points at the floor.

"The blood," he winces. "Wipe that up with something before someone sees it."

There is only about a half a cup of Bo's blood on the floor, seeping into the crappy beige area rug that your mom bought at Target but no matter how you look at it, it's still a half a cup too much for your taste. That rug has had so many pizzas, drinks and loaded bongs spilled on it that the stain is just blending in with the mosaic already there. *Why couldn't Bo have bled on the linoleum?* you ask yourself. Very convenient for cleaning up after a killing. A little Mop 'n Glo for Bo.

Hale reaches over to the pile of his clothes now on his bed and throws an old Billabong T-shirt on the floor. Although he looks the part, Hale Bernet doesn't surf. The shirt was purchased because it had the word "bong" in it. It's his favorite but he really doesn't seem to care.

You use your foot to wipe up what is left of Bo off of the floor with Hale's shirt. The guys just stand there and watch you, saying nothing. This room is usually full of all kinds of noise and this afternoon it's been one terribly uncomfortable silence after another. The fact no one is saying anything at all is starting to bug you, almost as much as the fact there is a corpse in your closet staring like a doll at nothing. You are starting to get impatient so you look over at Hale.

"Can we please light up now already?"

"Sure," he says. "But I think our dope is in the closet."

It takes you a full second or two to realize which dope he was talking about but sure as shit if it wasn't true. In the entire time you were hauling Bo across the floor and into the closet, nobody bothered to take your little baggie of weed out of his hand.

"Oh for Christ's sake," you moan. All of a sudden it feels like your head is way too heavy for your neck to hold up anymore. You know that nobody else is going to volunteer to open that door and ask Bo for your stash back. You brought it up so you are going to have to go and do it yourself.

You think you all almost half-expect old Bo to leap out of the closet the second you open the door, like in the movies when the bad guy isn't quite dead even though you've just shot him eighty-seven times and he jumps out for one last desperate lunge with his dying breath. You all expect that alright. Late night TV is much worse for you than a little bit of grass.

You open that door and there he is, just like you left him. He doesn't lunge, he doesn't make a peep, he doesn't do shit. He's still dead as dead can be. Gone, daddy, gone, and just as well because you feel far too drained at this point to have to kill him again. You know he looks like he's staring at you so you try to avoid his face. You just look for your stash.

It's there in his big ham-handed fist alright. You reach down and tug on it and it doesn't budge. You pull on it harder but Bo is determined to keep the dope to himself.

"I'll give up my Mary Jane when they pry it from my cold, dead fingers," you say to yourself thinking of that redneck retard bumper sticker that's probably on every other car back home. It's almost funny. You want to laugh but you are very afraid you'll just blow chunks again. Finally, you grab his wrist with one hand and yank the baggie free with the other. You can feel his cold skin under your fingers and smell the faint, sickly sour smell of the aftershave and sweat mixture on his body. You grimace and shut the door behind you. Skeletons in your closet alright. Wonder what the old man would think about this?

Mustering up your best pirate voice, you hold the baggie out for Hale. "Aarrgh, dead man's booty, anyone?"

They all wince at you.

You are turning into a real crack-up, a regular comedian. It's amazing what having a dead body around does for your sense of humor. He shakes his head and snatches the stash from your hand. You watch him load up and he passes the bong and the lighter to Nikko.

If there is anyone who needs the edge taken off right now it's

Nikko. He is one Ginsu knife motherfucker at this point and you almost expect him to bolt out the room yelling: "Dead body, dead body!" or some shit like that. If the Beckster was still around you'd score a Valium off her for him. But then again, you guess if the Beckster was still around then you wouldn't be sitting here with a dead Marine-wannabe in the closet.

When the bong comes around you don't bother giving Hale the high-sign, you just toke hard and instantly feel a hundred times better. You are starting to get hungry which almost appalls you at this point. A passing thought of Major Dick lying dead in your room shoves that pang away momentarily but the pot is kicking in again and the munchies along with it.

You wait for Hale to say something, to figure this whole thing out. That's his style, the scheme. You know you'd be able to put your two-cents in once the ball was rolling but you figure you should keep your yap shut until then. Even though it was you that swung the bat, you all tacitly know that you are all in this mess together. Self-defense or not, if you do your adds and takeaways your total still comes up in the red. You'd never be able to explain this away without seriously jeopardizing all of your futures. If you didn't go to jail, you'd surely get kicked out of school and you know that would be enough of an invite for your stepdad to clean your clock for sure. To clean it *Texas Style*. As it stood, you are royally fucked and at that moment you are praying to a God that you don't normally believe in to let you figure out a way to unfuck yourselves.

The past week you had been consumed by your depression over your breakup with Jackie. For close to two years you thought you were giving her what she needed in your relationship and you couldn't have been more wrong. She was there for you when you had your batting slump, she took care of you during the times when you were sick and all you ever gave her was grief in return. So of course, she left you so torn up over it that no one would have any trouble believing that you killed Bo because of it. Nobody.

Man, would her friends go hoarse from all of the "I told you so's" they'd give her and each other. They are such a bunch of jerks that they'd probably high-five each other for days on end after you got yourself arrested. For Christ's sake, all unshaven and dirty like this, you looked like a felon already. If Hale doesn't come up with something in the next ten minutes you are going to get in your car, drive to the airport and buy a one-way ticket to someplace where there is a Foreign Legion to join or a dense jungle to disappear into.

You wait for Hale to say something, anything, to save your collective asses. So you can imagine your surprise when it's not him who speaks up first.

"I have an idea how to get rid of the body," Nikko says, swallowing hard. "But you may not like it."

As it turns out, you don't. Not even one little bit. But deep down inside you have a gut feeling this is the only chance you are going to get.

3

You've been thinking a lot about Jackie and how your handling of that whole ambush would have sent General Custer into painful spasms of laughter. In your mind you go over all of the things you should have said to her when you were together. Shit, you know that saying about *hesitation and loss?* Well brother, you had both of them. Ha! Here you are, four feet away from a dead body that you are going to incinerate in a few hours, and all you can think about is the girl who broke your heart.

Nikko's plan is crazy. Not Jerry Lewis or Little Rascals crazy but plain old padded cell, loony bin, lock you up and shock your brain insane. As far as you are concerned, things in your life are pretty much hosed right now so how much worse could it be? Nobody comes up with a better idea for getting your asses out of this mess so you concede that you are in and so does Hale and Dan. You make a deal that you are going to stick together like flies on shit for the next few hours. Nobody smokes any dope and nobody leaves the pack lest they get second thoughts and screw the pooch. You are in this until the end, one way or the other. The plan is damned crazy alright, so damned crazy you think it might just work.

You wait until right before the dining hall closes to go down and eat so you'll be less likely to bump into anyone you know. Everyone around here hits the hall as early as possible, including Jackie and her pack of jackals, so you are more than happy to wait even though you are completely famished. Hardly a word is spoken by any of you during dinner. The rest of the guys mostly push their food around their plates, not eating much. You, on the other hand, eat like a condemned man, shoveling through three helpings of what appears to be Shepherd's Pie and a dry piece of chocolate cake. Usually the food here tastes godawful to you but today you'd think you had just been rescued from a deserted island and dropped off at the buffet table at Wolfgang Puck's house.

You throw on your baseball cap to cover your hair and with the exception of appearing a bit unkempt, you look fairly normal. You see a couple of guys you know but they don't sit with you and you are fairly relieved not to see any of Jackie's pack of bitchy friends either. That is the very last thing you need. The way you are feeling right now, one snide comment from any of them and you'd be liable to baseball bat the whole damn lot.

Your head is filling up with too many thoughts of a life that had just blossomed for you in the past week. A life that you hadn't exactly planned for yourself. The day-to-day existence of your world had been pretty mundane by anybody's standards. Six hours of sleep, ten laps around the track, too many classes, not enough base hits, not enough time to study, not enough time for your girl (obviously), three square meals a day and a good healthy bowel movement right after breakfast.

Every day was a carbon copy of the one before it and like any copy of a copy it was starting to dull around the edges a bit more as time passed. The problem was you thought you were unhappy. What a completely stupid jerk you were. You thought that your life lacked passion or flavor so you started smoking more dope. Well, *ya know why they call it dope, don't cha?* Ha, ha. Very funny, motherfucker.

You had it made. Your life was great and now it felt like you were watching a slow motion playback of you pissing it all away. Ladies and Gents, for your enjoyment please sit back and enjoy Scott Lorlon starring in Reefer Madness II: Body in Your Closet.

Your mind is swimming. You want Jackie back. You want this whole thing over with already. You want a joint. To break the monotony, you think of the most incredibly stupid thing that you could say.

"So, who do you think is more intelligent—dogs playing pool or dogs playing poker?"

Hale turns to you. "What?"

They all look at you like you must have just smoked a great big bag of crack so you ask it again.

"C'mon, more intelligent, dogs playing pool or dogs playing poker? You know, like in those paintings."

"That's the fuckin' stupidest question I've ever heard of," Dan says.

"Why?"

"You have to ask? Because, it's obviously those fuckin' dogs playing pool."

You don't buy his answer and Dan knows it.

"Well, shit man, it takes a lot more brains for a dog to use a pool cue, let alone know which ball to shoot at."

"A poker playing dog has got to know how many cards to deal," Hale jumps in. "Let alone if a straight beats a flush. A dog's more likely to sniff your crotch than know how to deal seven card stud."

Nikko is obviously disgusted by the stupidity of the whole conversation.

"I think," he says. "That you're all a bunch of retards."

Nobody says anything after that. You dump your trays and go back to the room. You check your watch every five minutes. Two a.m. can't come fast enough at this point.

There are hours to kill until showtime so Dan crashes out on your bed and Hale on his. Nikko goes to work on some sketches that you later find out are things you need to pull off Bo's disappearing act. Your neighbor, as it turns out, is one strange cat. He has always fancied himself some sort of covert secret agent wannabe so he throws himself into it. The funny thing is that Nikko is kind of awkward looking with the acne, bad posture and the Coke-bottle John Lennon glasses. You figure he's the last guy you'd ever expect to be a closet black ops kind of dude. Or would you? You guess the perfect guy is the one you never suspect. Right? You don't doubt he's smart enough though.

He is so into it that you wouldn't have been surprised one bit if he had thought out this sort of contingency way ahead of time. *What to do in case you have to get rid of a dead body* right there next to *Who to call in case of food poisoning* or *When your car breaks down on the highway.*

You want to make more stupid conversation to keep your mind off of things but think twice about it so you crack open a book for your Lit class instead. It's Joyce, whom you can't stand because it takes way too much concentration, but you are hoping that the density of thought power required to compute this bullshit will suck all of the other things out of your head for the moment. For five excruciating minutes you try reading and re-reading the first page over and over, trying like a madman to understand what it's all about. Instead, your mind starts drifting and you are thinking about Jackie.

She hated reading this awful crap as much as you did but at least she understood it. You really thought that she'd be able to help you through this class and at this point she'd probably be more likely to help you to a door slammed in your face.

It's nearly ten as you look down at your watch. Jackie should be just getting back from her dance class. You glance at your cell phone and it mocks you with its cold, plastic indifference. You could call to just see how she is, see if she misses you. The truth is she obviously doesn't. She hasn't called, stopped by, e-mailed or even heaved a rock through your window with a note on it. Fact of the matter, plain and simple, the ugly nugget of truth is that Jackie doesn't even miss you one goddamned bit.

The knock at the door startles you a little and you look over at Nikko. He's stopped working on whatever he's doing to look at you. For a second, you foolishly hope that it is Jackie finally coming to her senses to take you back. You almost don't want to find out though because the last time someone knocked on that door they ended up getting themselves a one-way ticket to Valhalla.

As you open the door slowly, you probably should have known it was going to be Hale's buddy Mitch. About the same time every night he came up to your room to glom some smoke off of you, so you started calling him Mooch instead.

Harmless enough, but he is a potential monkey wrench in the whole kitten caboodle. You know the best thing to do here is to get rid of him quickly.

"Hey amigo," he says. He calls everyone *amigo* or *compadre* which would be one thing if he were Mexican or Puerto Rican or something, but Mooch is a red-haired Irishman from Boston, as Mick as Mick could be, and his butchered Spanish can be pretty damned annoying when you aren't stoned. "Is Señor Bernet around?"

"Sorry man, Hale's kind of not feeling too good. He went to bed early tonight."

"Bummer. Hey, you got any chonger on you?" he asks. This pest is still willing to come in and smoke all over a sick buddy. You are starting to think that there just may be room in the closet for one more.

"Sorry, Hale smoked the last of our stash before crashing. He figured it would be medicinal."

"Right on. Well you never know when Major Dick may be right around the corner anyway. Someone should put a bell around that boy's thick old neck."

Man oh man. You get a big-league case of the creeps when he says that. You are trying to keep your poker face but you can feel your jaw clench up so much that you're afraid you'll bust your back teeth. It's time to get rid of this asshole. What kind of idiot still says *right on* anymore anyway?

"Yeah, man," you tell him. "Anyway, gotta study."

"Adios," he says but it comes out as *Ad-yoze.*

"Yeah, catch you later."

You shut the door. You need a smoke but you are going to keep your word. No dope until after the dirty deed is done. Over the past few weeks you have turned into a real pothead but you figure you'll worry about that later. You tell yourself that if you get through this you are going to toke your goddamn brains out.

Nikko starts packing up his little sketches and you watch curiously as he does so. He motions for you to come over to him.

"I have to run to my lab for a while," he whispers.

"What? I thought nobody leaves this room until it's time?"

You are feeling something akin to panic. Nikko is getting cold feet and ducking out on you. He plans to bail before the shit hits the fan.

"I know," he explains. "But we're going to need a couple of things to do this all with, and I'm going to have to step out for a couple of hours to put it all together."

You don't understand what he's rambling about. To you it sounds like he's going to get while the getting is good.

"Well, then let's all go."

"No, that would be too suspicious. I can get in and out of my lab and nobody would think twice about it if they saw me there."

"Fuck you if you're not coming back," you say. You don't know if this comes out like you mean it or not.

"Relax." Nikko puts a hand on your shoulder. "I'll be back in two hours. Wake those mopes up by twelve if I'm not back by then."

He grabs his stuff and heads for the door. Part of you wants to keep him from leaving, to stay here all together like you had planned, but you let him go anyway. He opens the door and looks back at you.

"Besides, I wouldn't miss this for anything."

And he's gone. You look at your watch again. Two hours is a

mighty long time to wait and see if your buddy is coming back to save your ass, or if he's decided to turn tail to save his own skin. There isn't much about this to like and you have enough on your mind to begin with. You keep thinking to yourself that Nikko wouldn't screw you over, that he'll be back with whatever magic beans you need to get out of this jam. Mostly you are hoping that Hale and Dan will either stay asleep until Nikko comes back or until you get freaked enough to sneak away to the airport.

The stress is getting to you. You are about one degree shy of a whole core meltdown of your psyche, hanging onto what little sanity you have left by the thinnest of threads. You have had enough. This is way too much for you. You are going to make a run for it. Fuck it all. You're a big goddamn coward. Admit it. You could be halfway around the globe in a straw hut on the coastline of some country with questionable extradition laws by morning. You are jumping ship. Your head is throbbing.

You sit down at your desk to write a letter to Hale explaining your chickenshit departure. You pull out a sheet of paper and a pen but the words aren't coming. You put your head down on your desk and start crying.

You wake up to the sound of voices. Your first thought is the police are here to take you to jail. You look at your watch—it's twelve-thirty. Nikko is back and he's showing something to Hale and Dan.

There was a dream about falling that you remember. You still have it every now and then. You're falling and falling off of a building or a cliff and every so often you see something to grab onto but it slips out of your hands. The ground rushes up towards you but you never hit. Maybe you catch your eyelid on a rusty nail to keep from splatting all over terra firma but you always wake up in time. You really hate that goddamned dream.

The note. Oh Christ. You remember the note that you were going to write. The paper is still there but it is blank. Thank God. You are still all in this together.

"Wake up Babe Ruth," Hale says to you, smiling. "It's time for a viking funeral."

4

The Towers are a pair of fourteen story, mid-rise, underclassmen dorms you can see from anywhere on campus. Now, if you had still been living there, getting Bo out of your room and into the back of Fuckin' Dan's Chevy pickup would have been futile. Tower North was an utter hive of activity all hours of the day and night and the chance of getting a body on the elevator without a hundred other people seeing was a practice in impossibility by design.

The first time you spent the night in Jackie's room you had at least a dozen people ask about it the next day. You could probably cart a dead body out of there on a Saturday night when nearly the whole place turned into a non-stop kegger and not a soul would notice. The system turned a blind eye to underage drinking in the Towers because it was the only way to make living there palatable. Sure the kids away from home for the first time would drink too much and alcohol poisoning and date rape would rear its ugly head every now and then. Your guess is that if you made the building dry, you'd have kids jumping off the roof, which you're sure would be viewed as much, much worse for business in the eyes of the college board.

This year, you are living in Stonehouse which is mainly a nice and quiet senior dorm occupied mostly by the voraciously studious, socially retarded and pure of heart. Mostly that is, which gave it the cachet of being Dullsville but it did have its perks. Two floors, bigger rooms, cleaner showers, good sunlight and better parking.

Hale drew a low number in the dorm lottery and picked room five, West Wing. It was one of the biggest rooms on the floor and for all intents and purposes, three people could live in it comfortably.

In a way, tonight you wish that he had picked room two instead. Though small and cramped, it has one thing going for it—proximity to the exit. You are three doors down. Even though that is only another fifteen feet, once you add Bo into the equation, it is going to be the longest fifteen feet of any of your lives.

The bright idea is that you are going to take Bo out the front door rolled up snug as a bug in your area rug, the very same rug that he bled onto. In theory, it seems like a great idea but when you open the door to the closet, you immediately get the sinking suspicion that operation Bo-be-gone is off to a very rocky start.

Rigor mortis has begun to set in and when you pull him out of the closet, Bo is bent like a boomerang.

Nobody had thought of this before so in your haste to get him off of the floor in the first place you pretty much just tossed him in there like an old blanket. Now he is all bent over with one arm kind of splayed to the side and you are pretty damn sure that you aren't getting him rolled up into the rug any time soon without a mallet and a hacksaw.

"Fuckin' fuck!" It's Dan's only comment but it says it all. You are sunk.

"Hold on," Hale tells him. And with that he grabs Bo's arm and tries to force it down into place. The sound reminds you of trying to twist the drumstick off of a whole roasted chicken. It moves but Bo's sinews are about as pliable as wood.

"Fuckin' fuck! Shit!" Dan howls again.

You start thinking about the airport again. You can say that you have to pee and just run to your car and keep going. It still isn't too late. Ten seconds into action and your plan just shit the bed. Goodnight Irene. You might as well just throw Bo over your shoulder and run around campus.

Wait a second.

"I got it!" you say. "Fireman's carry. Throw Bo over my shoulder and I'll do a fireman's carry with him."

"Someone could see us!" Nikko shrieks.

"Sure, but what if we throw a sheet over him," you say. "And then Hale throws a sheet over Nikko and carries him out over his shoulder. If anyone sees us between here and the truck it'll look just like any other evening with the four goofballs of Stonehouse."

"What about Dan?" Hale asks.

"Dan pulls the truck up, makes sure that no one's looking and lies down in the back. You dump Nikko and Major Dick in the back, Nikko and Dan get out. Switcheroo. It can't be any more suspicious than four guys taking a rolled up carpet outside after midnight."

"It's pretty fuckin' stupid, Scott," Dan tells you. "But we're running out of options so let's just fuckin' do it. Meet you guys outside in four minutes."

He's right, it is pretty fucking stupid. You probably can still roll Bo up like a giant rug cigar but what if you can't? It's already one o' clock and you need to do something quick.

"Jesus Scott, I hope you know what you're doing," Nikko says.

Hell man, that makes two of you.

You tear the sheet off of your bed and throw it over Bo. It isn't going to be easy carrying the dead bastard. The last thing you need is a goddamned hernia, you think. Nikko pulls Dan's bedsheet over himself. He looks like some sort of pathetic Charlie Brown kid at Halloween, like some pisspoor ghost. He still has on his knapsack with all of the goodies from his lab so he looks like a hunchback as well. In another situation it would be kind of funny.

Bo seems huge under your sheet. With the arm still sticking out a little he looks like a giant pile of rocks.

Hale helps you get Bo up on your good shoulder. There's no way he's two-thirty is your first thought. He's much heavier.

"Fix the sheet," you tell Hale.

He adjusts it to cover as much of Bo as possible. Skinny Nikko has room to spare underneath his sheet, but these are twin beds. With Bo you would need a Full or Queen size to do the trick. You have him up on your right shoulder but not too comfortably. You catch a glimpse of yourself in the mirror above your dresser. This sure as shit doesn't look too good alright, especially with Bo's arm hanging out part way to the side like a thick tree branch. Hale tries to cover it up but you know it will just come loose again anyway. Bo's boots are showing too but you don't care. Your reflection is beginning to look even whiter than the sheet.

The way you have envisioned it in your mind, it was going to appear like you are just carrying a sack of potatoes. Fat chance, it looks like you have a body draped over your shoulder, plain and simple. The rigor mortis has set in a way that looks awkward. A live person would just drape over you but Bo is bent. You balance him out the best you can on your shoulder but he is just way too top heavy. You feel something dig into your clavicle and start to think about Dan's boner-in-the-back story and shudder.

Please God, let that be a belt buckle, you think.

There is no way this is going to look any more graceful than a three-legged dog chasing a car. Your best bet is to jiggle him a lot so he looks something like somebody squirming. You were stupid to think that this was going to work but it's too late now. His weight is uncomfortable already and you aren't even out of the room yet.

"Let's rock," you tell Hale, but not as convincingly as you hoped to.

"Ready?" he asks Nikko.

Nikko nods through the sheet and Hale hauls him up over his shoulder. He slips a little and you think for a second that Hale is going to drop him.

You take a deep breath and turn the knob. You lean out and check the hallway. It is empty. The one thing that you can count on around here is most people are in bed by this time on a weeknight. After a couple of years of staying up 'til all hours of the night most folks start to learn the valuable lesson that sleep and defecation are the only true unalienable joys in life. Stonehouse is mostly quiet this way with practically all of the post-adolescent party goons living in the Towers or in frat houses. A Wednesday night like this around here is usually quiet as a church.

"Here goes nothing," you say to yourself and step out into the hallway. For a moment you are jerked backward and it startles you. Bo's splayed out arm has caught on the door jamb momentarily. With a tug you pull free. Hale comes out after you, shoots you a sigh of relief and you let him go ahead and walk point. Finally you are on the move. It is fifteen feet to the outside door and probably another fifteen to the truck. Less than the distance between third base and home plate but then again, you never tried it with two out in the bottom of the ninth with a dead Marine on your shoulder.

You aren't running; there is no way in hell you'll be able to, but you are going as fast as you can. The knee you bruised your freshman year starts to throb in a way that makes it painfully obvious it is the least happy joint in your body.

"Lord, please don't let anyone have to pee right now," you mutter.

At any point someone can open their door to go to the can and there you'd be. Howdy neighbor. Don't mind us. Coming through. You and Hale look completely ridiculous hauling two sheet-covered bodies over your shoulders but that's the point. In college, practically anything out of the ordinary looks only like juvenile hijinks to the casual observer. Just some kids having fun. As long as you are smiling, how can anyone be suspicious?

Hale gets to the outside door and uses his hip to open it. Nikko squirms a little and your guess is he's starting to get a little antsy not being able to see what's going on. Hale pokes his head outside and waves that the coast is clear before heading for Dan's truck.

"Almost there, hang in there buddy," you mutter, then wonder who are you saying that to? Nikko? Bo? Yourself?

You get to the outside door and all of a sudden you hear a noise from above you. The sound is unmistakable. Someone is coming down the stairs. Your ass is grass.

To the right of you is the outside, the truck, the escape— but if you try to make it out the door, whoever it is coming down might see if you aren't quick enough. You can make a run for it but Bo is getting heavier and then what if he slips out of your hands? You can't risk it. To your left are the bathrooms. You decide to hide in there until the coast is clear. Which bathroom though?

The ladies room is the closest. So you duck in there.

This isn't the first time you've been in the ladies bathroom. A couple of times, you and Jackie took a shower together in here. That was a lot of fun. Plus, the fear of getting caught was a giant turn-on to her. You did it in here because she thought it would be much cleaner than the boys room. You couldn't tell the difference. If anything, women were bigger slobs in the can than men.

You hope to God that nobody is in here already and luckily it's all quiet. You sprint for the back and hop into an empty shower stall and Bo's wayward arm gets caught again. With a quick yank you free it and pull the shower curtain shut. Turning around, you hear the muffled thud of Bo's head accidentally spinning into the tile wall. You groan. The sound is gross but as long as Bo isn't going to say anything about it, you won't either.

The bathroom is small and if your unexpected guest is female, you'll be pinched. Bo weighed way too much dead or alive and your arm is starting to numb too. You know you'll have to put him down really soon but if you do it in here you'll never get him back up on your shoulder again all by yourself.

A door opens and you barely catch your breath. The sound is too far away for it to be the ladies room door so it must be the other. You breathe a sigh of relief. You listen. A stall door closes and a toilet seat drops and hits the porcelain bowl. Whoever is in there is in for the long haul and you aren't going to wait for them. Stepping out of the stall sideways to keep Bo's arm from catching on the shower curtain, you sneak across the floor as quietly as possible. You have to go now. You get to the door and peek outside. Nobody in sight. Time to move.

You get outside and the truck is no more than twenty feet from you. Winded already and with your shoulder screaming, you catch Hale's "What the hell happened to you?" look and you do your best to shrug. It's the homestretch but it is a long twenty feet. You start to think you aren't going to make it. You start to think you'll trip on the sidewalk and knock yourself unconscious tumbling onto Bo's dead body like some halfwit gymnast. You start to think you'll wake up in a cell with some big fat sweaty biker trying to fill your dance card. You start to move your ass.

Ten feet... Five feet... Two feet... The tailgate is open and there is Dan lying there looking at the stars. He pokes his head up and grins at you. You tell Hale what happened and he just stares at you not saying anything. You unceremoniously shove Bo into the back of the truck.

"I think I'm going to have a fucking heart attack," you say.

Nikko is on his feet and has taken the sheet off. There are a few lights on but not a soul in sight. Dan gets out of the back and closes the tailgate. He looks at you, raises his eyebrows twice and slaps you on the back.

At first you think all four of you are going to cram into the cab up front but Dan doesn't think that would be such a good idea. First, his truck is a stick shift and second, if a cop sees four guys in the front seat he'll probably pull you over and that would just plain ruin the rest of your lives. Worse comes to worse, you can probably dispose of another body, but killing another witness is not something you can even begin to stomach at this point.

"We're riding in the back," Hale tells you.

"Why?" You think if this is a joke that it isn't very funny.

"Because Dan has to drive and Nikko knows where we're going."

You can't argue with that.

"Oh, and keep your heads down," Dan adds. "Riding in the back of a pickup is illegal in this town."

"Well I certainly wouldn't want to break the law now," Hale jokes. Dan grins at him. This is all very funny to these guys.

You climb into the back and lay down next to each other. You make him get in the middle. You carried Bo out here so your roomie can bump butts with him. It occurs to you that you aren't even sure where you are headed, not that it matters at this point. Hale puts his hands behind his head and looks at the stars. You do the same. It's a clear night over Los Angeles and you can see a lot more than usual.

Dan got himself a pickup truck so he could make a few extra bucks helping people move. It's a bumpy ride and after a couple of heavy jolts you grab a ratty old blanket and put it under your head. It's dirty and probably infested from sitting in the back of his truck but you don't really care at this point. Immediately, you start to get a little bit sleepy and feel yourself drifting off when you hear Hale mumble something.

"Dogs playing poker."

"Huh?" you ask.

"Dogs playing poker are smarter," he says.

"Why?"

"Teaching dogs to bluff would be hard."

"Not true, dogs always lie. It's in their nature."

"But bluffing and lying are like apples and oranges," Hale explains. "They both grow on trees but juice both of them and one looks like sunshine and the other looks like piss."

Hale says a lot of things that sound way more profound stoned than sober. Whatever he means by this is very lost on you at the moment.

"I guess so," you say. You feel like you have to say something in return. He looks to make sure you're the only one who can see. From under his shirt he shows you the butt of a pistol sticking out from the top of his jeans.

"Holy fucking shit!" you blurt out while he motions for you to shut up. Nikko turns around in the cab and you think he may have heard but he turns back.

"Is that real?" you ask.

Hale shakes his head. "My dad got it off the set of *The Great Escape*. Just thought it might come in handy."

You agree with him. You have no idea if he's telling the truth. It looks real as shit to you.

"Not your average Wednesday night in cowtown, huh?"

"No, certainly not," you tell him. "Certainly the fuck not."

It isn't a very long ride but by the time Dan pulls over and you poke your head up from the truck bed you might as well be on Venus. The school is surrounded by bad neighborhoods but this one looks like Fallujah. There are streetlights but only half of them work and you begin thinking that if those go out you'll probably shit your pants. This looks like it was one bad motherfucking neighborhood and you are four white guys that stand out like, well, four white guys in a bad motherfucking neighborhood.

Dan parks in an alley between two buildings and it smells like thousand year old piss. Gotta write home and tell the old man about this. No doubt about it, you are on Crack Street U.S.A.

The deal was to find a building that was abandoned and the one Dan picked certainly looks like it fits the bill. Shit, they all do. The place reminds you of how the Towers might look fifty years after the neutron bomb. You have to be the only people for blocks. No time to play Lewis and Clark though—welcome to Shitville, please visit our gift shop.

You want away from here pronto, brother. If all goes as planned, you'll be out of here in ten minutes max. You can keep your cool that long. You hope.

You drag Bo out and Hale pries open the closest door with a crowbar from Dan's truck. Nikko turns on his flashlight, hands you another one from his bag and you go in. You, Dan and Hale are dragging Bo by his arms. You look around. The windows all look like they've been boarded up for years. No one is going to miss this place at all.

Your adrenaline is going again. Here you are in the dead of night sneaking around some abandoned housing project so that you can torch the place. You'd never even consider coming down this street in the light of day, let alone the dead of night. It was scary as shit but you are jacked again. You all are. This is some real *Mission Impossible* type stuff and you are very into it now. No fear, no hesitation. You are hooked on the rush of it all and the more dangerous it gets, the more stoked you become. You have broken God knows how many laws—legal, moral or otherwise just today, and damn if it doesn't make baseball feel like washing the dishes.

The inside of the building smells like a combination of festering open sewer and rotting garbage. You try not to think about it. You think about how cool this place is going to look up in flames. Good riddance. You are almost sorry you won't be here to see it personally.

Nikko quickly finds what he's looking for—a bathroom. You kick open the door and the stench is overpowering. Someone has been in here alright, and not in the distant past either.

Without even seeing the belt around his arm or the needle in his hand you have a feeling the guy on the floor probably died of an overdose and most likely only a day or two ago at that. You shine your light on him and his eyes stare straight back, wide as saucers—as if he is surprised to see you, as if you had barged in on him. Part of his cheek is missing and your guess is that his face had become a snack for some rat. At least you hope it was a rat. This guy must have cooked up with toilet water, shot up and died right here in the shitter. Talk about a bad way to go out.

"The more, the merrier," Nikko says. He unzips his knapsack. He's really enjoying this. You drag Bo into the fetid bathroom and all together there are six of you in a can barely big enough for two.

You had seen the gizmo Nikko pulls out of his bag once before in your room about an hour ago. You didn't quite get what it was or how he was going to burn Bo up with it but you didn't think to ask then. You are very curious now though because you are rounding third base and you want to know how the hell to get home. To you the damn thing looks like a plastic mason jar full of something appearing to be kidney beans, with a nine-volt battery and a couple of wires attached to it. You have no idea that it is a detonator.

There is no doubt in any of your minds that Nikko is an evil genius of some sort. Here is somebody that you figure will either invent some kind of Nobel Prize winning box that was a boon to mankind, or just plain blow his fingers off in the basement. This is the guy who once explained to you how you could blow up your toaster with a strawberry Pop-Tart. You watch him set up the jar and check the wires. You hold a flashlight over his shoulder so he can see what he is doing. Damn if they really aren't kidney beans. Fuck. You were right. Magic beans.

He pulls a bottle of Evian out of his knapsack and pours it into the jar until it just covers the beans. He drops a metal plate over the beans and clips the wires in place. You are amazed. Mr. Wizard will now show you how to make your very own fireball using stuff from around the house.

"How the fuck does this work again?" Dan asks.

"Elementary, my dear dipshit," Nikko responds. "The water rehydrates the beans, the beans expand. The metal plate sits on the beans and in about two hours time the beans will have pushed it up so that it touches the wires where it completes the circuit between the battery and the ignitor."

"Ignitor?" you ask.

"It's an electric fuse for a model rocket engine," he explains. "So you can launch one of those babies with the press of a button from a battery operated controller instead of a lit fuse. It's really like a battery operated match."

"Where the hell did you learn this shit?" Hale asks.

"CIA Handbook. Bought it at Tower Records."

"Is that the one that tells you how you to get high from smoking dried banana peels?" you ask.

"No, that the Anarchist's Cookbook," Nikko says smugly. "I have both of them. Lots of great shit in there too."

He was beaming. Every boy wanted to be James Bond. Nikko wanted to be Q, that old guy who invented all of the killing toys for 007. You wouldn't be surprised if he wasn't already working on some sort of poison dart shooting pen or some shit like that.

Reaching into his bag, he pulls out a small plastic bag full of grey powder. For a moment you think it's gunpowder but then you remember how Nikko explained it earlier. It seems like a dozen years ago at this point but you remember it now. The bag is full of carbide which, when mixed with water, becomes acetylene, the gas they use in welding torches because it burns so hot. When Nikko's electronic match device lights up, this place is going to be one big goddamned clambake.

Nikko dumps the whole bag of carbide into the john.

"We're out of here," he announces, grabbing his bag and pushing you out the door. You are the last one out. You turn and look at Bo's body sprawled on the floor there next to some nameless junkie stranger. You toss him one final salute.

"*Ad-yoze,* Major Dick."

You shut the door and the four of you all run like hell for the truck.

Halfway to the door you ask yourself what in the hell you'd do if you got outside and Dan's piece of shit Chevy pickup was gone? What if you got outside to find that some low-life, crackhead car thief stole it? On a day like today, anything was possible and you are certainly the Murphy's Law poster boy du jour.

To your relief, the truck is still there in the alley where you left it. You look at your watch. You were only in there for five minutes but it feels like five days. Hale dives over the gate and pulls you in after him. Dan hits the gas and you are gone like the wind.

You keep your heads down in the bed of the truck but you and Hale feel like a couple of kids who just pulled off the biggest prank in the world. You laugh and high-five each other and you feel like someone has taken a lead apron off from around your neck. It is over. You are out of it. Even if Nikko's acetylene bomb doesn't go off and someone finds Bo they'd think the dead junkie killed him or vice versa. If it does go off, that building turns into a fireball and Bo becomes another burnt up body in a burnt out building. Put the pieces together. Sounds like the firebug got caught with his fingers in the pie, officer. There is just one last piece of the puzzle, one last card to play to make it all perfect.

By the time you get back, it's after two and you are beat. To say it had been a long day is a complete understatement of biblical proportion. All you want at this point is sleep and a whole shitload of it.

Dan parks the truck and you all get out quietly. He points at his watch and hold up four fingers. You nod but say nothing. You and Hale head back to your room.

Hale picks his bong up off of the floor and goes to light up. You are pretty sure that you want a toke but you need to lie down first. You take your clothes off and crawl into your bed. You are out before your head hits the pillow.

It isn't the fire alarm bell that eventually wakes you up at four in the morning but the pounding at the door. Hale is out like a light so you open the door in your underwear.

"Fire alarm man, gotta get out," says the cute girl from down the hall whose name is either Marcy or Matty or something. She is wearing a long T-shirt and you notice a tattoo of a frog on her ankle.

"Shit. Thanks," is all you manage to say.

You toss your bathrobe on, shake Hale awake and file out along with the other residents into the quad behind Stonehouse. You see Nikko on the way out and exchange "Heys". You see Dan across the quad and he gives you his *Shout at the Devil* bull's horns hand signal. You give it back.

Those guys don't come over, it's part of the plan. Dan had pulled the alarm himself. You wanted to make sure that everyone here saw the four of you at around the same time that Nikko's little do-it-yourself, instant-Bo-remover-in-a-can went off. Bada-bing, bada-boom, magic alibi and tons of witnesses.

A single fire truck arrives and within minutes you are allowed to go back in. You did it alright. You are geniuses; the whole damn plan worked like a charm.

But as someone once said, *Man plans and God laughs.* What you won't know until lunchtime was how funny this must have been to Him.

You wake up at ten the next morning having slept better than you had in days. Hale is still asleep so you grab your gym bag and head down to run your laps. Baseball season is around the corner and you have been neglecting your workouts. You are a little stiff today but you want to run.

After your laps you shave off the week's worth of growth and take a long hot shower. You look at yourself in the mirror and although your hair still looks like shit, Scott Lorlon is back. You plan to get your hair fixed later by someone who knows what the hell they are doing. First, you are going to wake up Hale and go chow. You feel great. You aren't thinking about Jackie. You aren't thinking about Bo. You are thinking about baseball, swinging that bat again and looking forward to all the monster dingers that you are going to hit out of the park this season. Maybe even make an effort to have the kind of season this year that gets you into the bigs.

When you get back to the room you find the guys huddled around the stereo. Nikko had been listening to the news all morning and when he heard what had happened, he came running to your room. You listen and wait and at the top of the hour it is the lead story. As soon as you hear, you feel your balls crawl up into your belly again. You had burned the building all right and they found bodies, four of them—all burned way beyond recognition. Nikko's firebomb worked alright, and along with everything else you burned up at least three other people.

This is bad. Very, very bad. The news says police are sure that it was arson, which means since it's an election year they'll be looking for the people who did it. Which means they'll be looking for you. Your balls don't like this one bit and they are letting you know it. And then come the words that you really don't want to hear.

"I've got an idea," Nikko says quietly. "But I'm pretty sure that you guys aren't going to like it."

5

"Great, so now I'm a fucking terrorist," you say.

Nikko is definitely one-hundred percent on target—you really don't like this plan at all. Congratulations, sir, you've hit the bullseye, win a fucking kewpie doll. You are not happy about this at all. Your good mood has snuck out the back, Jack.

"No," he tries to explain. "Well, not exactly. See the guys who firebombed the building are terrorists."

"That's us, isn't it?" you yell. This whole thing isn't making any sense to you at all.

"Technically, uh, yes," Nikko says. "But, if we make the police think it was some sort of terrorist thing it would throw them off of any trail that could possibly lead them here, to us."

Okay, it's slowly starting to sink in now. Bait and switch. Make the cops think it's somebody with an agenda. Who'd ever think to suspect a bunch of dopey slackers like you?

"How about a fuckin' militia group?" Dan asks.

"Man, you can get that CIA book anywhere," replies Nikko. "Maybe it's the same scumbags who burn down black churches or those bearded lunatics who hide up in the mountains and think the government is out to get them."

"Yeah," jokes Hale. "Welcome to Montana, at least our cows are sane."

"Nah, maybe it's some mailman going postal for getting held up on welfare check day," you say.

"Yeah, or some douchebag yuppie real estate militia trying to buy the land cheap and build a mall or high rise condo on it," Hale chimes in.

"Or maybe those fuckin' Young Republicans," Dan adds.

"I think it has to be a terrorist group," Hale says. "Militias are usually a bunch of fat, inbred, drunk, redneck cocksuckers."

When you were fourteen, your parents moved to a new house in a new town. You didn't know anybody. There was this bunch of guys who had kind of a "bike gang", and you started hanging with them because they played a lot of sandlot baseball after school and all summer long. It wasn't really a gang like in the inner city kind of way. You didn't carry knives or guns or deal drugs or fight anybody. You didn't really even care if other kids hung on your "turf". This isn't to say that you were a bunch of choirboys either though.

You'd go to the K-mart and lift stuff, mostly baseballs to replace the ones that you lost. Or, you'd steal sodas and donuts from the grocery store. Somebody would inevitably show up with a pack of cigarettes or a bone and you'd smoke that and every so often a kid would get real brave and sneak a Playboy or a bottle of hooch out of the house.

Aside from the soaping up of windows, toilet papering of trees and the occasional firecracker, the times you rode around at night shooting out people's bug zappers with pellet rifles, the afternoon you set that van on fire somebody said a homeless child-molester was living in at night, you never did anything too bad. You broke the rules that your parents had made for you, but wasn't that all part of growing up? It was a blast having friends like that. Guys who knew where the edge was and didn't think twice about giving it the finger.

You lost track of all of them when your parents moved again but you wouldn't be surprised if some of them were becoming lawyers or cops or firemen or criminals. Either way, you'd bet they'd be jealous of you right now if they knew what you were up to. You can bet your bike on it.

"Terrorists it is!" you say. "Let's smoke on it."

The stash baggie was low but you have more than enough to go around twice. You pass the bong and laugh.

"A friend with weed," Hale reminds you.

"Is a friend indeed," you reply back. You shoot him Fuckin' Dan's little hand sign and he sends it right back.

"Yeah brother," he says, sucking back a lungful from his bong.

"We, I mean, the terrorists, are going to need a name," you say, catching yourself.

"Why?" asks Dan.

"Because all terrorist groups have names," explains Nikko. "It's usually an adjective-noun kind of thing. Completely cornball though, you know, something that sounds like the name of a high school cover band or a dive bar in Hong Kong. Something that just sounds like a bunch of assholes."

"Yeah, something like Rising Moon," says Hale, still trying to hold in the smoke.

"Or Black Dawn," says Nikko.

"Or the Young Republicans," chimes Dan.

You all burst out laughing. What the hell? Why not blame it on someone else? The name should at least mean something, even if it was fictional. Terrorists, for the most part, gave their factions such obtuse and moronic names. You guess to them, the *Red*

Hand or whatever sounded lofty. To you, it sounds like something you get from jerking off too much. It sounds fucking stupid.

"Problem is," you say. "If we make the name sound religious or foreign, nobody will believe it was terrorists because the target won't make sense."

"Huh?" Dan asks.

"He's right," Nikko jumps in. "The slum building has no political or religious significance so why would a group that called itself the Monkey Nutsack Jihad or whatever firebomb it?"

"What if the reason wasn't political?" asks Hale.

"Or religious," you add.

"Or religious. Or what if it was kind of both but neither at the same time?" Hale asks.

If you weren't really stoned, Hale's statement wouldn't have made any sense whatsoever. But, in a very weird way, your corrupted brain cells fire their impaired synapses in a manner to know exactly what he means.

"Like what if it was the apocalypse?"

"Yes, totally, Book of Revelation shit!" he answers back.

"Holy Nostradamus, Batman. That's it!" Nikko jumps up. "What if whoever did it because they thought that the end of the world was near?"

"Wrath of God, day of reckoning," you say.

"Exactly!" says Hale. "Prophets have believed that the whole ball of wax goes all to hell at some point."

"Judgement Day. Tonight we're going to party like it's 1999," you say.

"Okay, but then, hypothetically speaking, what does Armageddon have to do with burning down a slum?" asks Hale.

"It's a crusade," answers Nikko. "You're trying to make God less angry. He gave us a world of beauty and peace and we've tossed it all away. Our selfish, shitty human nature has led us to poison our world, our hearts and our minds to the point of imminent destruction. In a time of hate and chaos and greed we've chosen to erase man's past mistakes by cleansing the world with fire."

You can't tell if he is serious or not. Hale actually looks a little frightened.

"Or maybe," Nikko adds, grinning. "We're just doing it to impress Jodie Foster."

You start laughing, mostly out of relief.

"I like it," says Dan. "I really fuckin' like it!"

A great name comes to you.

"We're the Doomsday Squad."

You are only halfway right. Hale gets that same look on his face that he had at the Omega Chi party with the Beckster's girlfriend. When he opens his mouth, he nails it.

"No, not squad. Way too fascist. It sounds like we're jackboot wearing, goosestep motherfuckers. We're the Doomsday *Club*."

Bingo. It's done. You smoke on it. Here you are back in your little bike gang world again and it is very cool. You are big-time digging it. There's always been mischievous blood in you from the time you were born, and the whole pseudo-terrorist thing fits you just like an old pair of jeans—once a troublemaker, always a troublemaker. You suppose a healthy aversion to authority will do that to you if you can avoid the constant ass-kickings that come with that sort of thing.

You stopped being a big Rush fan by the time you graduated from high school, but when someone knocks the first two bars of *YYZ* on your door you know it has to be Hale's pal, Carl.

Carl is a small time dealer. Grass, blow, ludes, a little X on Saturday night for those ratty little rave fuckers and sometimes 'shrooms and acid for the grad student crowd. He's a junior living in South Tower, has an iPod glued to his head nearly twenty-four-seven, and always has a parade of freshman girls coming in and out of his room. He's kind of a dirtbag, but Hale sort of likes him for some strange reason and the dude always has shit to sell you when you need it. The well is never, ever dry. On this campus, Carl qualifies as a natural resource.

The funny thing about Carl is that when you first met him he was all into Guns and Roses big time. T-shirts, posters, the whole deal. You even remember him wearing a bandanna wrapped around his forehead like Axl Rose. That shit was so twenty years ago even then, but you figured Carl probably came from New Jersey or Kansas or some lame-o place where chicks still wore their hair big and Bon Jovi could still get young girls wet by telling them how to live on a prayer.

When Hale first started buying off him, Carl wanted everyone to call him Slash, like the guitar player with the top hat. Everyone thought he was a dork and someone started calling him Snatch instead and it just kind of stuck. At first he was pissed about it, a real baby. But, after a while he started not to give a rat's ass what anybody called him, especially not his good customers. As far as he cared, you could call him *Nancy* as long as you had a stack of lean green dead prezzies for him.

Rarely, if ever, do you personally buy off of him, but Hale swears by Carl. Says his bags never come out light or get cut with anything too much to fuck them up. It's low grade crap to begin with, but Snatch sells cheap and pushes a fair amount to make up for it. He knows his market. These aren't kids looking for primo dope, it's all goofballs looking for a bottomless dimebag.

But to you weed is like wine. The better the quality, the more enjoyable it's going to be, and practically all of the imported shit kicks the piss out of any of that domestic garbage. Ninety-percent of Snatch's dope comes from South of the Border, which, when you live in L.A., is as imported as a soft taco. Your tastes lean toward the exotic, so when you buy, it's off of this kid Tom who's the equipment manager on the baseball team. A lot of times he gets this grass that he swears is from Thailand and nevertheless, is out of this world. Even though you know he does a little trade in 'roids with some of the kids on the team, Tom isn't really a dealer. He'll get some pot every now and then for himself and a little bit extra he hooks up a couple of friends with. You are on the top of the buddy list because you got him laid once at a room party you threw a couple of years back and you never let him forget it. It's a great arrangement, the only problem is that he wasn't getting it fast enough to keep up with your newly acquired smoking jones.

"Look, it's El Snatch-o," you say, opening the door.

"'Sup?" The usual Snatch greeting.

Hale opens up his wallet and buys two baggies of the usual Mexican Brown and tosses them to you to inspect. He knows it's halfway decent dope more than you do but you like to put on like you're the concerned shopper. You look in the bags, take a whiff and shrug your shoulders. Snatch shrugs back. What the hell does he care? You already paid him.

"I got something special today. That is, if you're interested," he says. Always the consummate salesman. This kid has a hell of a future ahead of him.

"Magic beans?" you ask, and Nikko shoots you a look across the room. Hale let out a chuckle.

"Check this out," Snatch says, digging into his pocket.

"Man, we're tapped," Hale tells him. "Cash flow low, amigo." He is bullshitting. Hale's dad sends him plenty of money but he doesn't want anybody to know about it so he keeps it on the down low. He thinks everybody will treat him differently. And you know what? He's right.

"Trust me, check this out," Snatch says.

He pulls out a tiny tin foil cube. You can't tell what it is until he starts to unwrap it.

"Hash, my friends. Straight from Turkey, the real deal," says Snatch. "It's part of my own personal stash but I figure you guys are good customers."

"Hey look, it's hash from Snatch's stash," you exclaim.

"How much?" asks Hale. He's kind of a sucker for a sales pitch.

Snatch gets up to leave five minutes later with his load a little lighter and his wallet a bit thicker.

Hale hides the hash in his desk drawer. He tells you he's going to save it for a special occasion.

No sooner do you buy then Hale's friends show up at your room. Word travels fast among the faithful and those needy of a good toke.

Mooch shows up first. He does bring his best party favor so you can't really say he arrived empty handed.

"Gentlemen, I bring you Salvation," he announces, closing the door behind him.

Salvation is what he's named his new bong and you can see it's a big motherfucker at that. Sixteen inches long, an inch and a half wide and completely hewn from neon green plastic. On the side he has painted the letters, S-A-L-V-A-T-I-O-N, in hot rod yellow. This is a pipe that just screams dope.

Another buddy, Rod, comes by on his way to make a beer run, and J.P. brings over a porno called *Taint Misbehaving* made up of really fat people fucking. It's the most hilarious thing you've ever seen in your life. You throw some cash together and order some pizzas and it becomes a party. It is late in the afternoon on a Thursday night, someone puts on the new Franz Ferdinand, cranks the stereo and you are starting the weekend early. This is the kind of shit that you came to college for in the first place.

6ix

By nine, the fiesta has broken up and you walk down to the TV lounge to watch *The Apprentice* with everyone else in Stonehouse. You have a small set in your room but this is a weekly event you enjoy. Besides, you had locked yourself up for the past week and you kind of want to be around people, even if most of them are just too fucking stupid to not talk during the show. What happened last night seems like a blur to you now. In a way, you can still feel it like an icepick stabbing into the back of your mind. You're sure that's why you chose to smoke until you couldn't think straight. Some demons are best left kept at bay.

Hale hangs back to call his little sister at Arizona State. He never comes down to watch TV. He calls television *chewing gum for the mind.* You never say anything but you have this sneaking suspicion he's watching *CSI* while you're down here.

Too late to get a good seat, you find yourself looking for floor space to park your butt into. Then it hits you. Just an hour before, everyone was having a good laugh at your expense. Your head still looks like you are having the supreme mother of all bad hair days. The show is starting and you don't want to run back to your room to get a hat. You just hope nobody notices, which is much like wishing they wouldn't notice you walking in with your dick on fire. There are a lot of eyes staring at you.

You sit against the big potted plant in the corner and figure you'll just sneak out after the show—kind of a bummer because you are in a socializing mood for a change. The thought of having to explain the sorry state of your hair to everyone puts a wilt in your boner real quick.

A couple of minutes later, that girl Matty or Marcy from down the hall comes into the lounge looking around for a place to sit and you can't take your eyes off of her for some reason. You guess you never noticed before what a great shape she has and the dark emerald green top she has on isn't hiding it at all. It looks tight enough to be a wee bit slutty without a hint of trashiness and you're sure you aren't the only one to notice this at all. There isn't any place else to sit so she comes over and joins you on the floor. She smiles at you and your mouth goes dry. Man, she isn't just cute, she's actually really pretty, bordering on knockout.

You want to think of a cool thing to say to her, something kind of Cary Grant. Your mind is coming up blank more like Pauly Shore. You are trying too hard but you're afraid if you just put the whole thing on autopilot you might go stupid all of a sudden and blurt out something like *Uh, your tits look great and I killed Bo.*

She kind of surprises you though when she beats you to the punch.

"Did I miss anything?"

"Yeah, the Donald's wig flew off and the guy who chased it down the street won immunity."

Fuck. Your brain is out in left field and you have no idea where the hell that came from. It's a real shithead attempt at a dumb joke.

"C'mon, stop pulling my dick. What'd I miss?"

Whoa. Hold the phone. You had never heard a chick say that before. Unless she was hiding something in those Levi's, you were pretty certain it was just a figure of speech. Hearing her say something almost dirty like that was kind of sexy. It kind of turned you on a little bit. You're a sorry twisted bastard, you suppose.

You say, "Sorry, I wasn't really paying attention to what was going on. I kind of zoned."

It was true. You hadn't seen what was going on because you were too busy gawking at her when she came in. You aren't about to mention that though. She smiles at you so you guess she doesn't think that you are too much of a dork. You really want to say something else but you decide to quit while you're ahead.

You don't speak to each other during the whole show although you want to. When it is over, she gets up to leave and you know you should try to at least say something, for God's sake. You can't be that lame, can you? The best you can do comes out of your mouth.

"Thanks for this morning."

"Huh?" She has no idea what you are talking about.

"The fire drill or whatever it was," you say. "Thanks for getting me up."

"No problem," she says. There goes that smile again. It is knocking you on your ass. "You wouldn't want to burn up or anything."

You are trying to swallow to get more, oh Christ, *any* saliva at all in your mouth and when she says that, you think you are going to choke on your own tongue, which at that point feels like a giant sandbag.

"Are you okay?" she asks.

"Yeah." You are coughing. "I was just thinking how awful something like that would be." You feel dizzy.

"Yeah, like those people in that crack building," she says.

Jesus. There's no way she could know about Bo. She must have seen it on the news or something. This chick is just kicking the shit out of you in every which way. You really don't know what to say this time. You just stand there with a stupid look on your puss. The scrambled jumble of works inside your melon is betraying you again. You think again about that little frog tattoo you saw on her ankle.

"Hey," she says smiling. "What the hell did you do to your hair?"

You try to explain it, minus the Jackie part, but you feel you are doing an extremely bad job of it. It feels like all of the wind has been knocked out of you. You think for sure she thinks you are a complete moron of some kind since your explanation stumbles into a mostly incoherent yammer of *uh* and *like*. To your surprise, she thinks it's funny. Some chicks are like that. Completely wacky in a very sexy way. You aren't completely used to it but you're sure you could get to like it. No question, you could get to like it a whole hell of a lot.

"Would you like me to fix it for you?" she asks.

Of course you say yes. It doesn't even occur to you that she might not even have the slightest clue as to what she's doing. You think about feeling her fingers running through your hair and you could tell *Little Scott* is starting to think that too. She could probably cut your ear off with a pair of scissors and you'd hardly notice at this point. Besides, you figure, how much worse could your hair look than it does right now?

You go back to her room and she pulls the chair away from her desk. The place is small with two beds kind of crammed on one side and two desks on the other. Certainly nowhere as big as your room. You and Hale would fucking kill each other if you were stuck in a joint like this.

"Where's your roommate?" You try to make small talk. You want to just put a hand on her cheek, pull her face towards yours and kiss her but you figure it wouldn't be the right move. Not yet at least. Kissing her is out of the question, at least for the next ten minutes.

"Jennifer? She's at the library studying."

It's amazing to you how many people share the same dull

routine day in and day out. Just a bunch of mopes sitting in the same building with their heads buried in books all evening. You never even talk to anyone over there and would be hard pressed to recognize anyone from the library except that fat girl in the wheelchair who ran over your foot one time and didn't bother to apologize.

There are framed snapshots on the other desk. Two girls, obviously drunk, whooping it up at a Halloween frat party dressed like Playboy bunnies. It's a Kodak moment alright. They are toasting the camera with plastic cups full of something. They look like they are having a great time.

She rummages through her dresser to find something and you realize you still have no idea what her name is. Damn, this is bad. You feel like a complete schmuck asking her, figuring she might get offended and hand you yet another dose of rejection. You sure as shit won't try to kiss her without knowing what her name is. Some guys wouldn't give a rat's ass but you know an opposable thumb is not the only thing separating you from chimpanzees. Being a dork or being a killer you can live with. Being a cad is out of the question.

But shit, you want to kiss this girl—and maybe more, but you are going to have to figure out what her name is before any of that nonsense. Mary? Maggie? Megan? Melanie?

Finally she finds what she's looking for.

An orange and white plastic rain poncho with a squinty and faggy looking vintage Tampa Bay Buccaneers logo on it.

"The Bucs?" you say. "An eternal optimist."

"I'm not really a football fan. I just have this thing for pirates. I'm afraid to wear a Raiders logo around L.A. lest someone think I'm somebody's *cholo* bitch or something."

Cholo bitch? Wow, wacky indeed. You summon up your best pirate voice.

"Aarrgh, ye matie, you need become a Pittsburgh fan."

"Steelers?"

"No, Pirates. Baseball, aarrgh."

"You need to work on your Captain Kidd, it kinda sucks

rocks," she shoots back, completely serious. You are shocked. You think you do a great pirate. Jackie always liked your pirate, at least she said that she did.

"It sounds like my grandpa with a bad case of hemorrhoids," she adds.

"Wow, I'm hurt." You clutch your hands over your heart. You are flirting way too hard like some dipshit teenager now but she obviously doesn't seem to mind.

"Chill out, Hamlet," she says. "Shatner would win the Oscar before you. Put the poncho on. You want more people to see you like that?"

Shit, the real question is do you want anyone to see you wearing a rain poncho? You put it on and feel like you're waiting for the short bus to school. But you figure that you're going to feel much worse if you don't divine what her damn name is.

She goes over to her stereo and picks through a small stack of CDs until she finds the one she was looking for. She puts it in and hits play and the soft sounds of Enya come out of the little speakers sitting on the floor. Jackie's big fat roommate, Liselle, had this album and you never remembered liking it before. It reminded you of something that you'd find in the background of some dumbass coffee commercial rather than real music. Tonight though, you're still kind of mellow from all of the dope, and in a way that you'd be ashamed to admit to the guys, you found it soothing.

"Don't worry honey, Manny is going to take care of you," she says, picking up the scissors and going to work.

Manny? Is that really her name? Isn't that one of those Pep Boys? The one with the big-ass cigar, suspenders and greased back, receding hairline who looked more like some alcoholic two-bit bookie than a tire salesman?

You look over at her and she bends over to look at what's left of your bangs, wiping them away from your forehead. A tiny gold charm around her neck pops out from the inside of her collar. It reads *Amanda.*

Sweet Jesus, that's a relief. For a while there you thought

about the *pulling your dick* comment back in the TV room and had begun to worry a bit. Hey, this is L.A. You hear about shit like that all the time.

You listen to the Enya, keep your yap shut and let Manny do her thing. It seems like she knows what she's doing and you aren't about to bust her concentration and risk a scissor laceration.

"The next time you break up with your girlfriend and you feel like doing your own hair, go get yourself a Flowbee," she says.

Holy crow. You didn't mention Jackie when you told her earlier about trying to cut your own hair. She knows though. Christ, everybody knows. The way people talked on this campus makes you sick.

"The truth..." you begin to say. The feeling is like hot, dry sand slipping through your fingers. The jig is up. You feel like a man too stupid to stop kicking a dead horse.

"...shall set you free," she responds, giggling. This is definitely flirting. Or is it? Your perception of reality has taken a hard one-eighty since yesterday so you aren't exactly so sure anymore.

You laugh. You think you should be going down in a massive ball of flames here and you aren't so far, so you laugh. It seems kind of stupid not to. Manny doesn't seem to care. She's too busy giving you a hard time about the tonsorial Hiroshima on your dome.

"Where are you from?" You try to escape from the whole Jackie issue. "I mean, like, where did you grow up?"

"A little town outside of Chicago called Wheeling." Manny pays more attention to what she's doing, which is good. "You'd have much better luck finding intelligent life up a dog's ass. How about you?"

"Houston, born and raised."

"Ahh, home of the ten-gallon hat," she says. "You don't sound like you have that speech impediment that passes for an accent in Texas." She breaks into a throaty Jack Palance. "Howdy, parrrd-ner."

"Actually I'm from a suburb called Kingwood. Home of middle class kids too disaffected and worried about nothing to really give a shit about anything," you explain.

"Sounds very Norman Rockwell."

"More like Norman Bates."

Manny giggles at this one too. You are definitely ahead of the count with more balls than strikes and are shaking off the bunt sign. If the next pitch comes over the plate high and fast you're swinging for the bleachers.

It feels good to flirt again. Flirt like you really mean it. All the time you were with Jackie you play-flirted with all of her friends and the occasional girl you'd meet during an away game or out drinking with the guys. It was fun then because you knew that it didn't mean anything. You loved Jackie and you'd never have cheated on her in a zillion years. The whole thing was just a game. Jackie did the same thing too and you were never jealous of it one bit. Problem was that you were too fucking stupid to be jealous because you never realized to her it wasn't really a game. She wasn't really playing. She was *Playing*, with a capital P. Hah, it shows you how smart your balls really are. They didn't know either.

"All done," Manny sing-songs in your ear. More like how you'd say it to a six year old rather than a college guy. Same difference when you really think about it. She points at the mirror on the back of her door. "Check it out."

Hey, your first thought is it's too short. But, you know what? It doesn't look too bad. It may not be the best haircut in the world but it looks pretty good considering what it was replacing. You can't polish a turd, but this was a thousand percent improvement. Running your fingers through it you decide it isn't a bad look for you at all.

"Wow, not too shabby, Gabby," you say, thinking some sideburns would look pretty hip with the new do. In a lot of ways, you are tossing aside the old Scott for some kind of as yet undefined new one, so why not?

"I like it," you tell her.

"My dad has a barber shop back home," she says, pulling the poncho up over your head. She opens the door and shakes your clippings out into the hallway. "He taught me how to cut his hair before I even had a training bra."

"That's because the wheels would get in the way." You catch yourself way too late to stop from saying it. Check you out. New haircut, same dorky brain.

"What?"

"Training bra? Wheels? Get it?" You are just digging your dork-hole deeper now. Man, are you an idiot or what?

"Oh," she giggles. "Don't quit your day job." So what if you're a dork. She brushes little hairs off of your shoulder with her hands and admires her handiwork. You should tell her you are much funnier when there is a dead body around.

"I'm afraid that I'm not much of a stylist," Manny says. "More of a barber."

She is right in front of you, her chest practically touching yours. Standing in each other's personal space and it doesn't seem to bother either of you.

"I'm afraid that I'm not much of a comedian," you say softly. "More of a dorky guy that wants to kiss you."

You cup her cheek in your hand and move your mouth closer to hers and she tilts her head slightly. The moment is only a fraction of a second away but the anticipation of the kiss is like ten thousand volts of electricity in the air. Your rush is coming back again. It feels like a freight train hurtling towards you. You can swear the hairs on your arm are moving.

Your lips touch for the briefest of moments, if at all, when the door opens. It is the roommate coming back from the library and she seems upset about something. Startled by the intrusion, Manny pulls away from you.

"You'll never believe the kind of shit Steve is trying to pull this time," says Jennifer. She looks up from her armful of books at you and turns. "Oh God, I, oh, sorry."

Sorry? You think to yourself. She ruins the moment you spent all this time setting up and all she has to say is *sorry*. Your rotten luck is like Domino's Pizza—bad and constantly getting worse.

You look at Manny and she just smiles. Is she bummed you

didn't kiss her or is she relieved? You can't tell. That's the problem with women. Sometimes they look at you like robots and you just can't tell.

"I should probably cruise," you say. You don't want to, but considering the moment was ruined you figure it's the best possible move on your part to avoid further embarrassment.

The only thing you can think to do is to smile at the roommate on your way out. It wasn't her fault. But damn, she couldn't have stayed at the library for two more fucking minutes? What a pill, no wonder this guy Steve was treating her like a doormat.

Manny follows you to the door and for a second you think she's just going to let you out without saying anything about what almost happened. You turn to thank her again for the haircut. This sucks. You still really want to kiss her.

"Sorry," she says.

There is something subtle for you to say rolling around in your head somewhere but you are trying way too hard to find it.

"Yeah," you finally respond. Damn, that isn't it. Can't you do better than that? Then it hits you from left field. "Hey, there's an Alpha Pi party on Saturday night. Wanna go?"

Okay, it isn't perfect but it's something. Not exactly a date but not exactly not-a-date either. Under the circumstances, it does seem a little bit wishy-washy.

Manny smiles. You are in. "Sure," she says.

"Cool," you tell her. You are about to wink but think twice about it.

You go back to your room and there is Hale sitting on his bed watching the ten o'clock news on the little TV. One thing seems a little strange though—the room is empty. This is usually about the time you'd come back from the library to find a couple of extra bodies in here smoking away. Tonight, nothing. Even Hale doesn't have his bong in hand for a change.

He looks up at you and it is very subtle but there is a bit of worry on his face. Worry mixed with something, boyish anticipation maybe. You can't tell but it seems like there is something on his mind. He checks out your haircut, probably wondering where the hell you got it at half-past ten on a weeknight.

"I liked it better the way it was," he says grinning. "You've lost that kooky shoe-bomber vibe you had going there for a while."

"Manny cut it," you tell him.

"Who the fuck is Manny?" He wrinkes his nose. "You mean that completely homo custodian guy with the limp?"

"No, loser." You know who he's talking about. Some guy with a full-on Freddie Mercury moustache and a club foot who works for the college. "I mean Amanda down the hall in seventeen."

"Brunette. Great rack, killer smile?"

"That's the one." You shoot him Dan's little hand sign.

"Dog," says Hale. "To think I was saving myself for her."

"Snooze, you lose, vagrant," you beam.

"You'll let me get sloppy seconds, right?"

"Hey man," you tell him flatly. "Once you've had an arsonist, you never go back. Speaking of which." You point to the set.

"Nada," replies Hale. "But I turned it on late and could have just missed it."

"Let's hope not."

You are seriously hoping the whole thing is going to be just forgotten. There isn't a chance in hell of that though. You just have to wait until morning to see what is going on. You tried to forget that little pinch you have been feeling in the back of your mind all day, but now you can feel it messing with your head again.

You sit through the sports, the weather and a story about some dumbass dog that chased a rabbit into a storm drain and got stuck until some firemen dug him out. Happy ending for the dog but it isn't exactly making you feel any better. Yesterday you could tell without a doubt what that dog must have felt like, trapped in that drain. You feel your chest tighten up a little bit.

Hale turns off the TV, turns on the radio and dials in the all-news station. Reaching over to his dresser, you pick up his bong, just wanting to take the edge off. You light up the residue in the bowl then hold it out for Hale but he shakes you off. Can you remember the last time he turned down a toke?

The news starts and you get butterflies in your stomach. It feels like you are waiting for your name to be called. Your hit hasn't kicked in yet. You are hoping there isn't another war in the Middle East or anything. Not for humanitarian reasons mind you, but because you don't think you can sit through more than five minutes of waiting without your head just exploding.

You don't have to wait too long at all though. It's the lead story. It seems like a gob of fiction spewing forth from the female reporter's mouth. You have to remind yourself that it is all too real. She says...

"...death toll is up to five tonight in the fire that leveled an abandoned South Central apartment building. Police searching through the wreckage today located what they believe to be yet another body on the first floor. Four other bodies were found on the second floor earlier today and are originally thought to be the only victims in an early morning blaze that police suspect to be arson. So far, none of the victims have been identified."

You look at Hale and he is just staring at the speaker. All you can think to do is pace back and forth across the room. It isn't hard to tell that you are both thinking the same thing.

Five.

The new victim had to be Bo, or was it the junkie? Either way, why didn't they find both? The news this morning didn't mention anything about them, only about finding bodies on the second floor. That meant that all total you had torched up six people, at least two of them dead beforehand.

Your head is reeling as if someone is beating you with a big rubber hammer. The news makes no mention of terrorists but then again, why should they? You never made any effort to tell them that it was. The four of you came up with that great plan and didn't bother to pull off the most important part. The trail could find it's way back to you and it would be pretty damn stupid to think that it still wouldn't.

And that's when your cell phone starts to ring.

7

Immediately you think it has to be the cops closing in on you. *Hello, Scott Lorlon? Smile jackass, we've got you surrounded. By the way, nice haircut.*

There you are standing right next to your phone and all you can do is watch it ring.

"Scott," Hale says.

"I don't want to pick it up." You can tell by the look on his face that he is getting a bit aggravated.

"For fuck's sake."

He gets up off the bed and walks toward you. When he gets to your desk he looks at the phone and then at you and you think for a second that he isn't going to get it either. After the third ring, he picks it up.

"Hello?"

Somebody on the other side says something and Hale just grunts. Before you can ask who it is, he hangs up without saying goodbye or anything.

"That was Nikko," Hale tells you. "He says he's going to his lab right now and we should get a good night's sleep. We'll all meet here for lunch to talk about stuff."

Lunch? You'll meet for lunch? You are possibly on your way to getting big time royally fucked and these guys are treating it like a game. Bucky and Chad and Chip are going to come by and do lunch about the whole bomb thing. Hell, are you the only one that gives a shit about this whole fuckball? And what the hell is bomb-boy doing running over to his lab at the moment you should be discussing how you are going to handle this? Are you crazy to be worried?

"Scott."

"Huh, uh, what?" You are spacing out again.

"Relax, man. Relax."

Maybe you are making too big a deal out of all of this. If anyone had made the truck at the scene it would be a different story but there wasn't anything in any of the news reports about possible suspects or witnesses. In a neighborhood like that, what are the chances anyone seeing anything is going to tell the police jack shit? You had to be smart enough to not get caught. Most criminals are stupid. Not you guys.

Hale is flipping through the AM dial, trying to find the story on another newscast but all he can get is Mariachi music. You are feeling the need to get out of here for a while. Get away from this room, this building, this campus. It is time to just get into your car and just drive the hell away from here for a little bit.

Opening the closet door for the first time since yesterday, you grab your jacket. You think you catch a faint odor of Polo but shrug it off. Your jacket hangs on the back of the door and you grab it off the hook. There is a bit of a chill in the air, but honestly you are more interested in what is in the pockets than you are in keeping warm.

"Be back later," you tell Hale. He waves, not even looking up from the TV.

The Civic hatchback is old but runs great. You bought it two summers ago and drove it cross-country yourself. Your folks didn't think it was such a great idea but that never really stopped you before. You took a week and made an effort to see as much of the west as possible, which isn't really a whole hell of a lot in some parts.

There is always enough parking behind Stonehouse so you usually take the same space in the back by the lot entrance. You walk past the collection of other vehicles parked there, a little more than half are older pieces of junk like your Civic. Some ragged and rusty, dented and dinged and looking like they are enjoying their last waltz before the scrap heap. An old Datsun here, a Volvo in a color that nobody's seen brand new in ten years there.

Mixed in with these hulks are the new and nearly new

Nissans, Beemers and the occasional Mercedes belonging to the progeny of the rich. Being wealthy or not neither made you more of a prince or an asshole than the other guy. You walk past Hale's Camry—it's a nice car but he hardly ever uses the damn thing because he is embarrassed by it. His dad bought it for him when he got to college and you know if it were up to Hale, he'd drive it down to Huntington Beach and trade it to some surfer kid for a beat up old VW van all covered with peace signs and skateboarding stickers.

You unlock your door and get in. You catch what you think may be the slight scent of Jackie's perfume, *Miami Glow*. You are probably imagining it. Your second olfactory hallucination of the evening. The ghosts of perfumes past coming back to haunt you. Wonderful. You key the ignition and the engine starts up smartly. You put the car in gear and you are gone.

There were a lot of drives like this with Jackie, especially when you both lived in the Towers. Sometimes it was the only time you'd get to be alone without all of the interruptions of phone calls and roommates and stereos blasting from across the hall. The car was your place. It was where the two of you went to get away from it all and just be yourselves.

You had a bunch of special places that you'd go together. Your favorite was this tiny park off of Mulholland Drive that looked out over the lights of Hollywood and that's where you are headed. For a moment you wish Manny was in the car too but you need to go there yourself and reclaim it for you first. That park is going to be your special place now. Jackie isn't going to take that away from you too.

The road winds up the canyon into the hills. You pass one gigantic home after another and you think of how Jackie always wanted to know who the hell lived in all those ridiculously expensive houses. Real estate out here was so pricey you always wondered what in God's name you have to do for a living to afford a joint like that. Someone told you Jack Nicholson lived on Mulholland somewhere which would answer at least one of those questions.

As usual, the park is empty. You pass a couple of other cars stopped at one of the other lookout points down the road. The view isn't as good there but your guess is those other folks aren't here for that. You put it in park and go through your jacket. At first you can't find what you are looking for but in one of the inside pockets your fingers close around it. You pull it out and look at it for a while, rolling it between your fingers.

It is the one of the joints you had rolled with the Thai stick that Tom had sold you. You always kept a little stash away from Hale that you'd only share with Jackie. This was the last of it and it was going to be a ceremonial smoke on your part.

Clicking on the dome light in the car, you take your wallet out of the back pocket of your jeans and dig out the picture of Jackie that you've carried since you started dating. Although it is something you see every time you open up your wallet, you can't remember the last time you sat and stared at it. You think about the day you took this picture at the zoo. You had just eaten lunch and were holding hands on your way to see the polar bear tank. There were these three statues of a mother bear and her two cubs in the pathway and Jackie just ran up and leaned against them and you snapped the shot. In that moment, with the sunshine in her face and a slight breeze tousling the bottom of her sundress, you knew you had fallen for her.

"The last of the best," you say to yourself sticking the joint in your mouth. You aren't exactly sure of what you mean by that. Maybe you mean to say it the other way around? You shrug it off. Whatever.

You light up and suck back a hit. You get out of the car and walk up the embankment and sit on the ground.

Your throat feels pretty harsh from all of the smoking you've already done today but the Thai stick is much smoother than the shit you got from Snatch. You know you are smoking way too much dope lately but it is helping you through this rough patch. Life is getting way too fucking hard and you really need it to keep your sanity from taking a holiday. You are feeling like a train that has been derailed. Screw the world if it frowns on your smoke break until you get back on track. You'd go back to Coach Riggs and beg your way back onto the team. That would keep you focused until graduation. You can keep it together until then. Piece of cake.

You look down at the millions of lights twinkling below. You try to remember a story that always makes you realize that it could always be a *lot* worse.

Hale has an older brother named David who was marrying this girl he had been with for a really long time. There was a big church ceremony and the girl's parents rented out a hotel ballroom for a reception for some hundred and fifty guests. So, right after dinner, David gets up, takes the microphone and starts to make this little speech about how he was really happy that his family could be there and that the bride's entire family could come in from out of town and all of her friends and that his best friend since high school could be his best man today and so on and so forth.

He's smiling and going on about how great it is for everyone to be present on this occasion to celebrate this special day together. So, as a token of his appreciation he tells everyone that he's taped a special gift for them underneath all of their chairs. A little something that would make sure that they never forget this moment.

Now, about two months before the wedding, David got a whiff that his fiancee might have been unfaithful to him so he hired a private dick to follow her around and find out for sure. Well, it turns out that the cheating bitch was screwing some other guy and the P.I. got pictures of it. So, when everyone reached under their chairs they each found a manila envelope containing an eight-by-ten glossy of David's fiancee leaving a Motel Six with her secret boyfriend. The very same guy who happened to be sitting next to David. His best man. His best friend.

David waits as a collective gasp fills the room. He then turns to his new bride and says "Fuck you," turns to the best man and says "Fuck you, too," drops the mike on the floor and walks right out the front door and gets the marriage annulled the next day.

Now, you've got to admire David's balls. Here's a guy who knew that his wife to be was cheating on him for months, even had the proof for Christ's sake. Most guys would have broken up with the girl and beaten the crap out of the best friend but he had the ultimate revenge. He waited until after the ceremony and humiliated her in front of her parents, grandparents, aunts, uncles, cousins and friends and waited to do it after her dad had already paid for everything. A move as brilliant as inventing the Polio vaccine.

David didn't even care that his family was embarrassed as well. Not too long afterwards he quit his job, packed it all up and moved to Amsterdam and now edits copy for an American language newspaper over there. Hale gets a letter from him every now and then. The last time he wrote, he said that for the first time in his life, he was happy.

You take a last drag on the joint and crush the roach under the heel of your shoe. Your watch says it's almost one o'clock. You are getting sleepy and it's time to head back. Back in the car System of a Down comes on the radio and you turn it up as loud as it'll go and scream along with it.

8

Around eleven, you wake up and the room is empty. Hale has left the window by his bed cracked open slightly and it's fucking freezing in here. For some twisted reason you are angry at the window for being open. You know it sounds completely stupid but you are. The goddamned window is pissing you off and you spy a sneaker under your bed and want to throw it at the window, to hit it and let it know how angry you are with it. With your luck you'd end up breaking the damn thing and Lord knows, as far as shit goes, you have a full plate already.

You look at your watch and are surprised at how late you've slept. Once again, you are missing your Friday, ten a.m. Lit class but it's okay because you still haven't read more than the first page of the piece of shit Joyce book that you were supposed to have finished by today anyway. You'll have to start going back to class soon though but the hell with it, you'll deal with that after the weekend and that's what Cliff's Notes are for anyway. Procrastination—the American way, goddammit. You start thinking about Bo and the fire and the faceless people you burned up and your head begins to throb. The last thing you need at this moment is a dose of reality ruining a reasonably good morning. You try to convince yourself you don't really care.

The guys aren't going to be coming by for about another hour so you toss some stuff in your gym bag and head out to do your laps. Your throat feels like an old ashtray no one ever empties so you grab a Coke out of the vending machine. The carbonation tastes like burning rust in your throat but your body soaks up the sugar and the caffeine like a sponge. Your energy gauge gurgles up a couple notches and you think to yourself on the walk over how a Snickers would have gone down pretty smoothly too.

Right away, you know you probably won't be able to make your usual ten trips around the track. Your legs feel stiff and the knee you used to hold Bo up starts to ache after the third lap. Man, that dead jackass is probably going to mess up your chances of making the team again and you'll end the season riding pine, in the bleachers. You had stretched before running as always but probably not enough since you were in a hurry. The pain gets worse so you quit after an uninspired effort at a fifth lap. No doubt about it, the pot is taking its toll on you already. This is *so* not good. In your present condition, you'd need to get yourself high on adrenaline before every game to be in shape to play. You joke with yourself that you don't think there are enough people around here you'd really want to kill to be able to pull that off.

Disgusted with your pathetic self, you quit for the day and head for the showers. The hot water feels good on your stiff muscles and you stand there for a long time letting the needles of spray hit you in the face. The tenseness you feel is sapping your strength on top of everything else. The semester just started and you already need a break again. It isn't too late to get it all back in sync though. At least not yet, you hope.

Your mood picks up a little when you get a good look at your hair in the mirror. Damn if Manny hadn't done a pretty decent job. Yeah it's much shorter than you are used to but you guess she had to do that to even it all out after your crappy hack job. You are digging it. It looks less Texas and way more California. You think if you bleach it out and put a guitar in your hands you'd look totally MTV. You do a Pete Townshend air-guitar windmill in the mirror and shoot yourself a Dan hand sign. Maybe you'll scrape up a few extra bucks and get some peroxide and a pair of wrap around shades after lunch. Or a tattoo? You are feeling pretty badass, why the hell not? Something like a lightning bolt or a skull or maybe a row of five little stick figures of people like the way fighter pilots mark their kills on the sides of their airplanes. How about a dog playing poker? Okay, it's going to take some thought. The only thing worse than a shitty tattoo? Two shitty tattoos.

Back at the room Hale is reading the paper which would normally seem kind of strange. As long as you've known him he's never seemed to take much of an interest in current events unless it happened to be a Warped Tour or a big pot bust. It's obvious what he's looking for though. When you are a current event, you guess it's only natural to take an interest.

As you had feared, the story is plastered all over the front page. The finding of a new body and a particularly slow news day probably kept it from getting buried ten pages back. If there was one day that you needed a Tsunami or a Rodney King beating in your life it was yesterday and the big G. has let you down.

There is a picture of the burnt out shell of the building and with the exception of soot and smoke trails from the windows and a mostly caved in roof, to tell you the truth, the damn thing looks nearly the same as you left it. The story says the flames gutted the old building within minutes.

There isn't much more in there you don't already know from last night's news. Five bodies, still unidentified, and only one, so far, found on the first floor. No suspects but police are indeed talking to eyewitnesses of the blaze. Nothing about four dope-smoking college jerks in a white pickup truck. Not so far.

You look through the college paper and, not surprisingly, there isn't anything on Major Dick's disappearance. Why would there be? He wouldn't be officially gone for forty-eight hours until today and anyway, this was California. Here you almost come to expect someone is going to flake on you and not show up for a date or a class or a meeting or whatever. But this isn't a surfer dude or valley chick, this is a Marine and most of them are just obedient machines programmed to be on time. Hell, most of them wouldn't even know which end to shit out of if a superior didn't tell them. They are too mindless to flake. Bo's being AWOL is going to get noticed soon enough if not already. Even if they never I.D.'d Bo's barbecued body from the fire, someone may get around to putting two and two together and come up with four. Four skunk smoking jerks in a white pickup truck, that is.

Nikko and Fuckin' Dan show up separately about five minutes later. You turn on the set to catch the news at noon and there is nothing new to report. At least it has been replaced as the top story by yet another high speed police chase on the 405. You feel a little better about that. L.A. is the kind of place where anything at all could happen at any minute and you are praying someone will go out and do something much more terrible than you just to take attention away from the damn fire.

Dan skims the article in the Times and hands it to Nikko who shrugs it off since he's already seen it. You are all on the same page as to what's happening here and you are guessing you are just going to just sit and wait until this whole thing just blows over.

Boy, are you wrong as wrong could be on that one.

"The paper says that the fuckin' police have eyewitnesses to the blaze," Dan says, mostly to you.

"Eyewitnesses to the blaze, which probably means people who saw the building on fire. Not necessarily anyone who saw anything beforehand though," replies Nikko.

"Yeah, but we really don't know that for sure," Hale adds. It's a good point. You have absolutely no idea what anybody saw or when they saw it. The unspoken agreement in the room confirms you are all thinking the same thing. Somewhere on the other side of town, some crackhead or some kid may have seen the truck, one of your faces or the whole damn thing. Cop cars could be on the way here right now for all you know. Aw, Christ, if you hadn't burned up all those other people you'd probably believe this was actually all over.

You speak up. "Yeah, but what about the whole 'only one body found on the first floor' thing? Correct me if I'm wrong but I distinctly remember seeing two bodies."

"Yeah," blurts Dan. "That's fucked up."

You direct all of your questions to Nikko. It's almost like it is his press conference. You guess since it was his bomb, he'd have all of the answers.

"I was thinking about that too," he says. He speaks matter-of-factly, in a way that reminds you of Robbie the Robot from *Lost in Space*. "The news last night said the police found *the remains* of what they thought was another victim on the first floor. That bathroom was ground zero of what should have been an incredibly hot fireball. Bo and that junkie should have completely vaporized. Your guess is that they found no more of either of them to fill a lunchbox with. They just think it's one person. They'd have better luck trying to I.D. a dog turd."

You'll be damned, the little firebug did have all the answers. And if not, you'd just as soon believe the ones he had already.

"What if they aren't completely vaporized? What if they find teeth?" asks Hale. "Can't they I.D. someone by dental records if they have an idea of who that person was."

Hah, you knew it. He was watching *CSI*.

"Yeah, what about the fuckin' dental records?" Dan chimes in.

"The fireball at the source is going heat the pulp up in a tooth to where it'd just pop like a chestnut."

"Are you sure?" you ask.

Nikko doesn't have the answer to that one. At least not the one you want to hear.

"That's why I brought this," says Nikko. He reaches into his knapsack, the same one from two nights ago, and pulls it out. Your heart misfires like a bad engine when you see what it is. It is almost as bad as if he had pulled Major Dick out of his bag.

There in his hand is another detonator just like the one from two nights ago.

What the hell have we started? you think to yourself.

This is one sequel to a bomb that you don't want to see go into production but it is too late. Lights, camera, action. You start to feel as if someone has just stopped payment on your reality check.

"Whoa baby!" Hale blurts excitedly. His eyes light up and he takes it from Nikko's hands. You knew it; these guys were loving the big game.

You look at the detonator and don't understand what it's doing here.

"Why?" you ask.

"Because—" he starts to answer but Hale interrupts him.

"Because now we've killed enough people that the police aren't going to be satisfied to let this case go unsolved."

"Right!" Nikko nods, agreeing with Hale. "They're going to follow any lead they find and if they happen to tie in the sudden disappearance of a college student to the same time they may come sniffing around here."

"We have an alibi though," you sputter. "The fire alarm. Everybody in Stonehouse saw us."

"Yeah, but we don't really know exactly when the bomb went off," Nikko tries to explain. "My best guess is the beans took two hours to set off the fuse, give or take twenty minutes or so. Even though we were all seen here at four in the morning, the alibi's about as airtight as a screen door."

"Fuckin' fuck!" Dan exclaims.

"We've got to throw the cops a bone that they'll follow in the wrong direction. By the time they figure it to be a dead end, school will be over."

It makes sense. If the cops go off thinking it was some bunch of loonies that did it, they might investigate that angle for months and end up chasing their tails like a pack of monkeys. Better yet, they'd toss it to the FBI and it would get bogged down for even longer. You could stay clear long enough to graduate and be out of here entirely. Any Bo trail would be pretty cold by then and they'd have a pretty hard time linking anybody to anything.

The problem was simple. The first bomb was supposed to get rid of Bo's body or at the very least make it look like he had gotten himself killed trying to get his junior arsonists merit badge. Unfortunately, no one foresaw you'd end up killing a bunch of other people who were unlucky enough to be crashing for the night at the Hellfire Hilton. The worst part was that you couldn't be sure nobody had seen you. You set this thing in motion and now you are going to have to see it through. There was just no way that after all of this shit you were going to jail. Not for one death and certainly not for five. For all you knew, the other bodies could have been more dead junkies. You weren't going to ruin your life because they were too fucking stoned to get off of the tracks before the train came through.

"So now what you're saying is that we have to set off another bomb," you say.

"No, not exactly," says Nikko. "I'm not too terribly keen on killing more people."

"I think we reached our quota for this lifetime," Hale adds.

"Then what?" Dan asks.

"We set up the detonator to go off and then call it in as a bomb threat before it goes off," explains Nikko.

"Cool," Hale says. "I get it. The cops show up, disarm it easily and no one gets hurt."

"The caller takes responsibility for the first bomb too, right?" you ask.

Hale puts his fist up to his face like he's making a phone call and pinches his nose with his other hand. "Excuse me officer, do you have Prince Machiavelli in a can?"

Nikko keeps talking.

"Right, and when they actually find a bomb they'll be inclined to believe that the whole thing is the sick and twisted work of someone or *someones* calling themselves The Doomsday Club," Nikko says. "Bada-bing, bada-bang and Bob's your uncle."

"Wow," you say in utter disbelief. A bomb scare. The idea couldn't be any more stupid than throwing a sheet over Bo and carrying him out on your shoulder. This whole thing is about as serious as a cupcake.

"Maybe I'm a fuckin' dope but why do we have to use a real bomb then? Why not just call in a fake bomb?" asks Dan.

"Because," Hale answers. "They need to find a device like the one that could have torched that slum building. Then they'll think the lead was real and off they'll go down the garden path and away from us."

You are impressed. Your situation has continually gotten worse and somehow you've managed to keep from getting bitten in the ass by staying one step ahead in the little game you have devised for yourselves.

"Maybe I'm fuckin' crazy but I don't mind the bomb so much as I mind going back into that neighborhood," Dan says.

"I agree," says Hale. "We have to hit another type of target. The hood is too suspect now anyway."

You can think of a bunch of places that could use a good blowing up. Man, you'd be bound to get a writing cramp that list would be so damn long. Problem is, most of these places were on campus which would be like inviting the cops to crawl up your asses with a microscope.

You think if you were a cop and something blew up on your beat, the first place that you'd go to would be the nearest college. It is the way obvious choice in your book. Cops are such dopes though. Give them half a chance and they'll want the excitement of busting the big one that gets their faces splashed all over the front page of every fish wrap in the state. Get them jazzed that it's terrorists and they'll make it be a bunch of terrorists regardless.

The next target has to be big. The kind of big where the cops who find the bomb get treated like heroes. Dinner at the mayor's house, key to the city, ticker tape parade, guest shots on *Good Morning America* and *Leno*. The kind of big where it looks like they saved the lives of a whole shitload of people.

"A bank," you say.

"Too difficult and they have security cameras," Hale shoots back.

"Department stores, too," Nikko says. "So that's out."

"And malls," you add.

"Yeah, but I fuckin' hate malls," Dan says.

"A mall," says Nikko, rubbing his chin. "That would almost be like a public service."

"A restaurant," Dan says. "One of those fuckin' chi-chi places on Melrose or Rodeo."

"Oooh..." You can tell Hale likes the idea by the way this comes out of his mouth like he was admiring a big diamond or a pierced nipple. To him, a yuppie target would be like striking back at his own folks. You can see him picturing his dad sitting down with a big greasy mouthful of veal picata when the fireball hits. He is chuckling.

"Yeah, we could do that," Nikko says pensively. "Thing is, we need a source of water in a closed and undisturbed room to keep the acetylene gas in. The smaller the better, that's why bathrooms work so nicely."

"It has to be exact even though we're not going to set off the bomb?" you ask.

"Yup." Nikko sounds kind of annoyed as if you should already know the answer.

It is a stupid question. The whole thing has to look as right as rain. If it doesn't appear to be a totally righteous setup the cops would smell a phony a mile away. You have to play this one exactly as if you are doing it for real. That, you are afraid, is the real danger. Knowing you don't have to really set off the bomb makes it more likely you'll end up getting yourselves caught because you were sloppy.

After this stunt, you are out and back to your drab and silly little lives. Although it is exciting being an ersatz terrorist. You are pretty sure that what you really need is a semester of worrying about the inside fastball, getting yourself laid and not having to look over your shoulder every ten minutes. This whole mess is real close to being over and you have to see it out until the last hand is dealt. If you blow it now, you'll all go to jail and you are perfectly happy with keeping your asshole the same size it already is, thank you very much.

"It may be too hard to rig," Nikko shakes his head. "How do you keep people out of the bathroom if the place is open?"

"I got it," Dan answers. "Go in there and sling some chocolate pudding all over the walls, then go tell the manager and they'll shut the can for the rest of the night."

"Ladies and Gents," says Hale. "The long lost child of Mr. Magoo." He starts clapping.

"Fuck you very much," responds Dan.

Picking on Dan once you got him going is a favorite pastime in this room. You have something you always love saying to him.

"Speed kills, Dan."

"Fuck you too, Scott."

You are going to suggest you all need a toke to jump start the inner terrorist in all of you. Your throat still feels like shit from being the human pot chimney all day yesterday though. You'll never be able to sit there and watch them smoke without you.

"Okay, then how about an out of order sign?" Dan says.

"Huh?" asks Nikko.

"Out of order sign," Dan repeats. "Men's room out of order, kindly go fuck yourself."

You look at each other. He has something. It isn't the complete answer but you are getting closer. All those years in school, learning to read, learning to add and learning to do, are marrying everything you've been taught in the movies by the Cages, the Diesels, the Connerys. Trying to plan a real terrorist attack was proving extremely difficult. It made all of the Joyce, the Fluid Dynamics, the fastballs seem about as complex as the recipe for an ice cube.

This is all doing something to you but you're not sure what.

You know you have somehow changed from the Scott Lorlon who wore this skin just a few days ago. The boy has been shed off. It would be hard to say there is now a man in its place but instead maybe an older boy, a tougher boy. A boy now ready to someday become a man. But not yet. It is the boy in you, like all boys, who enjoys thinking of the excitement of the rush.

You suppose that's when you know you've grown up. When the rush stops being important and instead you care more about just keeping what little you've managed to accumulate, the boy in you has flown the coop. The day that comes is the day that part of you dies. Congratulations bud, you've hung up your hunting horn and become a nester.

Of the four of you, you are hands-down the biggest wuss of the whole group. There's no way you could have kept out of this kind of trouble yourself. You'd probably never be in this kind of trouble yourself but that's the point. Your life, by your own design, is so middle of the road, so bland. Vanilla ice cream without hot fudge. You've always seeked out the bad influences to follow because it kept things interesting. College was going to be the last big party because that's what your parents had drilled into your head. This is your last semester. This is last call. A year from right now you'll be stuck in the first of forty years of nine-to-five, client meetings and morning traffic.

The thing is, there's still a whole lot of dumbass kid in you. It's the part deep down that cares more about where the next party is than where your future is. The part of you that is willing to wager your life against the hollow promise of the rush. The part of you that is unable to hold onto the best thing to ever fall into your life. The dumbass kid still in you wants badly to be part of this now more than ever, because pretty soon it will be too late to be anything other than you, and that is scarier than anything else you can imagine.

When you were younger, you moved around a lot and didn't really get the chance to make the kind of friends a kid needs growing up. There wasn't anybody that you'd known longer than high school that you still kept in touch with and every holiday season there seemed to be fewer names on your Christmas card list than the year before. Hale, Nikko and Dan were undoubtedly the best friends you've ever had in your life but it took you until now to figure that one out. Sticking together through this whole thing just went to show you how close you had become. Friends help you move, real friends help you move bodies.

The idea is slick alright but there are way more variables involved here that needed filling in. You'll have to pull this off in the light of day and doing that without drawing witnesses is the real sticky trick. There is no longer any doubt as far as you are concerned— you have a real sick, twisted head full of works. You feel like there isn't any kind of problem here you can't come up with an answer for. There isn't a time that you can remember that you've gotten this excited about anything.

It starts to seep into your head that school is utter bullshit. They give you this rosy-ass picture of life and sucker you into believing that all the answers can be found in books somewhere. That's a major league load of grade-A, hot, steamy crap. Now you know that most of the time in life you're going to have to go out and find all the answers yourself and the world will be more than happy to just bone you in the ass if you don't. The room has become a cacophony of madness, with all of your sick and genocidal musterings romping in your minds like a psycho-savage ballet. There is no blueprint for the insanity you've created so you close your eyes in the smoky room and improvise.

"We need a target first. We can't make an effective plan without a target," says Hale. He is looking at his watch and you can tell what he's thinking. All of this black-ops stuff makes a man hungry.

You break for lunch. On the way to the dining hall you bump into some guys you know from the team and start talking shop with them. All of the bomb talk has stirred a strange primal feeling inside of your head and you need to get yourself grounded again by thinking baseball again. They talk about a scout who came by practice the other day.

These guys are saps, you think to yourself. Some fucking people are so unrealistic about their chances in life. Just because you are the best whoozit in your small pond back home doesn't make you shit in the real world. You are starting to believe that balls and brains will get you through life a lot better than a handful of talent.

You get to the cafeteria and the line is a bit longer than you thought it would be. Usually you'd bitch about something like this but today it seems too trivial to matter. Out of the corner of your eye you see two of Jackie's crummy friends gorging themselves on ice cream from the sundae bar. You are hoping they don't notice you, but it's too late. They keep looking over, whispering to each other. It is completely ridiculous and entirely beyond getting on your nerves. They have to be two of the phoniest bitches you could ever meet. The kind of skanks who'd probably trample each other trying to get the other's boyfriend. You could never stand either of them anyway. It's people like that who make you think the gene pool could benefit from a healthy dose of chlorine. You start to wonder if you could bean both of their empty skulls with a dinner plate from here.

Wolves always travel in packs since they're too afraid to go out alone so you are almost certain that Jackie is around here somewhere. At the same time, you want to see her but you are deathly afraid that you won't know what to say to her. It's a big school but you run in too many of the same circles to keep avoiding each other. Take this dining hall for example. It's the closest to Stonehouse and to Park Hill, her dorm building, and all of your collective friends eat here. You'll be damned though if you were going to start eating on the other side of campus and run like a dog with your tail between your legs. It's not like she hasn't embarrassed you enough already, so in a sick way, it's more fun to see them squirm not knowing what to say to you. Fuck 'em all, you know who your friends are.

You are so distracted by your thoughts that you don't even notice your teammates have been griping to one of the servers about the lack of meat on today's lunch menu.

"Hey, what gives?" one of them is yelling. "I didn't fight my way to the top of the food chain to become a vegetarian."

"Yeah," says the other teammate. "Any chicken in that kitchen?"

It never ceases to amaze you where inspiration comes from. Sir Isaac Newton was sleeping for God's sake when he created his theory of gravity. If that apple hadn't fallen on his head we'd probably walk around believing that the earth just sucks, which is truly an arguable point as far as you are concerned.

Your honor, just look at me, you think. *I rest my case.*

As it turns out, just by listening to these two idiots piss and moan about the menu, the absolute perfect target comes to you in a flash.

9

Although it's not home to the kind of big movie stars anymore as is neighboring Bel Air, Beverly Hills was still the crown jewel in the cultural pomposity of Los Angeles. One time you were in the car with some guys you used to play ball with and you're driving through on your way to a party some actor buddy of someone's is throwing. All the cars around you are Mercs or Porches or whatever, and in a white convertible in front of you there's this couple that looks like they just stepped out of the middle of GQ Magazine. The guy behind the wheel was just tooling around without a care in the world with some fashion model looking chick spoon-feeding frozen yogurt to him while he's driving. Pretty much the life wouldn't you say?

You pull up behind him and you're just watching the show, totally jealous. You get to a red light and standing there is this homeless guy, all ragged and dirty and looking like the whole entire world had just chewed him up and spit him out right there on the corner of Wilshire and Doheny. Mr. And Mrs. Perfect were done with dessert and were more content to sit there making kissy-poo when this homeless guy comes up to the car looking for change. The guy in the Benz takes one look at this poor bastard and you know what he does? He hands him the unfinished cup of Haagen Daaz. It was probably only going to melt all over the leather seats anyway, right? It was the most arrogant thing you'd ever seen in your life. Anywhere else you would have been shocked but in this zip code it shouldn't really have surprised you one bit.

So, in a bizarre way, Beverly Hills is to L.A. what Times Square is to New York—a cultural icon of extremely questionable integrity that scores a big meatball in the redeeming social value column. You're not too certain though if the peep shows and titty bars of Forty-Second street are any more obscene than a nine hundred dollar Gucci purse or a two thousand dollar dinner jacket at Barney's.

Rodeo Drive is as much a tourist trap as is Disneyworld. Every designer with a name worth a shit has a boutique and every boutique has a salesperson with an attitude that desperately makes you want to believe that they really don't want you to spend your money there. It's a bizarre world as foreign to most people as is fisting or bumper pool.

Go one block over to Beverly Drive and you've given up Louis Vuitton and Tiffany's for Starbucks and The Gap. As a mortal, you are more likely to comprehend your surroundings and maybe even find something for sale that won't cost you a week's pay. On this street you'll find a deli and a Blockbuster and a restaurant with valet attendants that won't laugh at your car if it cost you less than sixty grand.

The weather is cloudy but warm and mild and, best of all, the traffic is light. You turn on KLOS and Zeppelin's "Misty Mountain Hop" comes on and you play all of John Bonham's drum fills note for note on the steering wheel. You sing most of it over to Nikko and he looks at you like this trip can't be over soon enough. Some people have no appreciation for music. Goddamn peasants.

You don't tell Nikko where you are going and he's getting

impatient. Unlike yourself, Nikko goes to all of his classes and the thought of maybe missing his next one, the lab with the cute co-ed T.A. he was always gabbing about, was making him nervous. You don't know why he even cares, he's too shy to ask her out anyway. Besides, she's probably sleeping with a prof which certainly happens a lot in your school for some reason. Whoever said T.A. meant Teaching Assistant?

"Hey," you say to him. "Chill, okay? We're almost there."

Nestled here is Chicky's Chicken Kitchen. A nice little joint with great sandwiches, big salads and best of all, public bathrooms. The kind of bathroom you can just walk in off the street to use. As long as you don't look like a vagrant or a supermodel, no one will even notice.

After lucking into a great parking space a block down, you drop a buck-twenty-five into the meter—twelve lousy minutes per quarter. Street Parking is pretty scarce and the only alternative is a six-dollar lot and you aren't about to do that. You have to save your money for important things like books and pizza and dope and bombs and shit like that.

Although you are almost too poor to even window shop, you and Jackie would come down to Rodeo every now and then. She liked to look at the clothes and you would sneak looks at the rich and beautiful women buying thousand dollar cocktail dresses the way you'd buy a bottle of Heineken at the Key Club on a Saturday night. Every now and then she'd see a suit or a shirt that she said would look good on you. Your sense of fashion ended with knowing to wear pants with cuffs that touched the tops of your shoes. You didn't know chic from shit. You were happy just getting your clothes at the Gap where everything just sort of goes with everything else like Garanimals for grown ups. You always had a feeling though that people who could afford to shop on Rodeo generally weren't any happier or, more appropriately, less miserable than you.

On one of your little field trips, you discovered Chicky's. The food was great and being able to say to her dopey friends that you had dinner in Beverly Hills was always fun for a laugh or two.

They all had boyfriends whose idea of a romantic evening was a six-pack and a lot of groping in front of the TV before the game came on. It's not like those girls deserved any better though.

You buy two Teriyaki Chickywiches and two Cokes while Nikko goes to the bathroom. Grabbing a booth in the rear, you sit with your back to the wall. You count five people working here. A couple of them even look illegal. In this neighborhood? Don't even think twice that it couldn't happen.

The only thing funky about Chicky's is that, like a few places in L.A., the bathrooms aren't in the restaurant. You have to get a key from the register and go next door to a hallway that separates Chicky's from a joint called The Bagelry in the same building. Most likely just the doings of some cheapskate landlord saving a few bucks by making them share with the place next door. Nikko gets the key for the Men's and disappears though the hallway door.

A few minutes later he comes back smiling. He pulls out a pen and starts making notes on a napkin. You don't say anything, just keep quiet and eat your Chickywich. Every couple of minutes or so, Nikko takes a huge bite of his and chews it slowly, even methodically, while making more nearly illegible scribbles. You can make out a rough sketch of the bathroom's layout but that soon is covered up by the storm of calculations rolling off of his pen.

You drain your soda and go back to the self-serve fountain for a refill and that's when you notice a security camera high on the wall pointing right at the door. You look around and don't see any others. Most fast-food type places have something like this so that if someone robs the joint they'll be caught on tape coming and going.

Instead of saying something about it to Nikko when you go back to the table, you just watch him stuff the last giant bite of Chickywich into his mouth. That's Nikko's way of eating. Some people who are incredibly smart usually have weird personal idiosyncrasies that make them a bit uncomfortable to be around sometimes. Take Bill Gates for example. The guy's some sort of wicked computer genius but for the life of him can't figure out how a comb works. Nikko eats with all of the subtlety of a steam-powered trash masher and frankly, it's kind of fucking disgusting.

"Let's go," he says with his mouth full of half-masticated Chickywich. "I have a three o'clock."

You're not sure if he even really cares about the class so much as he wants a good perch to stare at the T.A., who, in his words, has *the ass of a goddess*. If it were you, you'd probably fail that class for sure, too busy staring at her bucket the whole time. You don't have the heart to tell him that the prof is probably nailing her.

You want to say something about his godawful eating habits but decide against it. When you have friends who play with sub-atomic particles for kicks you tend to let matters of etiquette slide sometimes. It occurs to you the only thing the two of you said to each other during lunch was him telling you that he wanted to leave. Eerily, this reminds you a bit too much of your last lunch with Jackie before she dropped you like third period French.

The meter says you have twenty-five minutes left which means it's shorting you by at least ten.

That settles it, you think. *This piece of shit town deserves a Nikko special.* You are already about to leave but then it hits you about the security camera. An idea comes and you tell Nikko to wait here for a minute while you run to Banana Republic. Once before with Jackie, she found this funky shirt that she wanted you to get but you told her it looked stupid and ended up hurting her feelings. Besides, it was sixty-five bucks, which was a hell of a lot more than you could spend. You couldn't believe that she'd get all bent over a stupid shirt.

You find it on the same rack in the back where you had first seen it. Grabbing a medium you go to the register and pay for it with the Visa card your parents gave you for emergencies. They'll give you shit for this but you'll get out of it somehow. You'll tell them that your jacket got stolen and you needed a new one or something. Did it even matter? They'll probably come out to see a home game at some point and ask to see the jacket and you'll play dumb and say "what jacket?" and they'll yell at you. It doesn't seem fair that life has to always be an endless raft of shit from your folks.

The skinny model-type at the register barely smiles at you as she rings it up. Why should she? It's not like you are Brad Pitt or anything. Though you are pretty sure if you were, you'd hardly even smile at her either.

The people who work in these stores amaze you, always acting like they rank up there with the Mother Teresas of the world on their own personal "love me" meter. Hey, cure cancer and you'll be impressed but ringing up purchases probably makes you just another bitter jackass with a bad headshot and no SAG card. You watch as the clerk folds the shirt neatly and puts it into one of those shopping bags with handles on it. This is what you came for, the shirt is just a bonus.

Nikko leans up against your Civic and appears annoyed again. He looks at the bag and points.

"Don't worry," you tell him. "You'll thank me later."

The whole way back he can't stop talking about what you need to do to get the bomb into Chicky's. It seems like a lot and you aren't exactly getting it all but you are jazzed again. Scott Lorlon, secret agent, covert ops, reporting for duty. Now if you only had a secret compartment ring with a joint in it and a Ferrari to pick up some women with, you'd be the man for sure.

Back at your room alone you light up Hale's bong by yourself and turn on the stereo. You leave your new shirt in the Banana Republic bag and put both in the closet on the floor. The weather report calls for brief afternoon showers which isn't too unusual for February. A Ben Folds song you aren't quite sick of yet comes on and you turn it up louder. You take a toke and try to hold it in through an entire chorus.

Pot does strange things to you. After the bowl you pick up that Joyce book and plow through a large chunk of it. The weird thing is, not only does it all sink in but you even start to enjoy it a bit. Being stoned is probably the secret to understanding whatever the hell that man was trying to write. You think maybe next week you'll smoke some crack and try to read some Camus.

When Hale comes back you are asleep on your bed with your beat up copy of *The Portrait of an Artist as a Young Man* open on your chest. You think you may have dreamed that you were Stephen Dedalus saying goodbye to everything he held dear. You aren't sure if it was that dream and not the naked-picnic-with-Whoopi-Goldberg one you've been having lately.

"Scott."

You open your eyes and Hale is standing by the open door, looking out into the hallway. When you get to your feet you can see that a lot of other people are milling around the hallway too. At Bo's door is a Marine in uniform.

Your first thought is that it's Bo back from the dead.

A creepy feeling comes over you, starting at your shoulders and going down to your asshole which is puckered so tight you think you might lose your balance. Gut instinct is a reflection of anxiety but pucker factor is evidence of pure fear.

The thought that they never found his body in the building because he had somehow gotten out flashes through your head. You are spooking yourself for no reason. This guy isn't Major Dick. First of all, he's much bigger, taller. Second of all, when this guy turns around you can see he has a chest as wide as a picture covered with a rack of ribbons. This guy isn't Bo. The star on his shoulder lets you know this guy isn't just any ordinary jarhead. This is the Head Jarhead.

The custodian at his side fumbles through a giant ring that looks like it holds every damn key to every damn lock in the world. Nervously, he tries to find the one that goes to Bo's room. He looks like some sort of ex-con to you and the thought he had possible access to your room doesn't instill any kind of sense of security. You remember you haven't seen your hiking boots in over two weeks and let it pass. You check out the custodian again. He looks familiar but you don't quite place the face until you see the name "Manny" on the patch on his workshirt.

You glance over your shoulder and there is the other Manny, Amanda.

"Nice hair," she says, shooting you a wink.

Wink. She winked at you. You knew you should have winked at her last night. You're such a complete dork when it comes to women. Some guys are real smooth and have all the moves and slick things to say. You? You're just happy if you can carry a conversation with a girl without making her think you have some sort of head injury.

"You like it?" you kid her, running your hand through the new do. "If you want, I can recommend my stylist."

"Barber," she corrects.

"What's the difference?"

"Oh, about ten bucks and a lot less staring at your ass when you leave the shop."

"Isn't there someone who will stare at my ass for less?" you kid.

There goes that smile again. It's enough to almost knock you off your feet. She stands there right in front of you, rocking back and forth on her heels with her hands in the pockets of a pair of faded jeans. Your mind once again falls into blankness.

"What's going on?" she asks.

"Uh, not much. How about you?" you say. It isn't what she was asking though.

"No, silly. What's going on at Major Dick's room?"

You laugh. Everyone called him that behind his back.

"Don't know." You are trying your best to be convincing. "Maybe he's spying for the Cubans."

"Maybe he was abducted by aliens," she jokes.

Holy shit. That'd be a great one. Bo kidnapped by a UFO. They'd have a blast running tests on him. Maybe they'd even take him back to their planet to mate. Oh man, like that wasn't a frightening thought—a race of Bo aliens. That's what you should tell everybody. That he left on a probe for Uranus.

"Jennifer said that nobody's seen him in days," she adds.

Days? That's a bit of an overstatement but so be it. Let

Manny's roommate and everybody else think Bo flew the coop a week ago for all you care. At least twice a year you hear about a kid dropping all of the sandwiches out of his or her basket. Most lose their shit entirely and have massive stress attacks from all of the pressure of school and dating and whatnot. Some try to kill themselves. Some succeed. Sometimes other people miss them when they're gone.

You watch the other Manny open the door to Bo's room. He and the Marine take a couple of minutes to look around before they come back out and close it up again. The Head Jarhead thanks the custodian, and for a second, you think Manny (the custodian) might just salute him. He doesn't, at least not before the Marine leaves Stonehouse.

"Do you think that was Bo's commander?" Manny the fair asks.

"Who? General Knowledge there? Maybe he's investigating the abduction for the White House UFO committee," you tell her.

"You're bad," she says, putting her hand on your chest.

"You have no idea." You wink at her.

You want to take her out tonight but she says it's a friend's birthday and they are all going scorpion bowling to celebrate. You laugh. Lest anyone think it involves poisonous arachnids and ten-pound balls, scorpion bowling is a hallowed tradition around here that one participates in on your twenty-first birthday. Hong Kong Harbor is a polynesian restaurant and bar that has incredibly lousy food but first-rate mixed drinks. The most famous being a near-toxic concoction made up of eighty ounces of no less than a dozen different types of alcohol. It comes to your table in a gigantic half coconut shell full of fruit and paper umbrellas and ten straws. It's called a scorpion bowl but they might just as well call it *The Regurgitator*. Your guess is they make it with the runoff from the rubber mat the bartender pours all of the other drinks on.

Wishing her luck, you hope she'll be over her hangover in time to go to the party at Alpha Pi. Just as well, because tonight, you and the boys have a bomb scare to plan.

You go back to your room and Hale gives you that "you sly bastard" look. You caught him staring while you were flirting with Manny. The best part was you knew it was killing him how you had picked her up without even really trying.

"Yeah, bite me," you tell him.

"My brother! Back in the saddle!" He gives you a hug.

You sit through five excruciating minutes of a *Friends* rerun waiting for the evening news because Hale has left the remote on top of the set and neither of you are motivated enough to get up and get it. You could be six inches away from the set and still use the remote instead of reaching over.

A promo runs and you can tell the top story this hour is going to be about a chase on the 405 this morning. They have lots of helicopter footage and the money shot of the guy rolling his Datsun three times. Last week it was some disgruntled ex-city worker who stole a bus and ended up plowing into the side of a house in Lynwood somewhere. You are pretty sick of the same old shit, you want the big story. The meat. The chewy center of the Tootsie-pop.

After the chase it's a gang shooting, then a bank robbery. You are probably next but you are dropping out of the public eye. You wait for your fire but the next story is about a truckload of livestock that overturned on the freeway down by John Wayne Airport. It's funny to you that Orange County named their airport after a dead movie cowboy. Looks like they could have used the old Duke today to ride around and rope all of those little porkers. There are pigs running free into traffic getting hit left and right.

Hale laughs. "Man, did you see that?"

Christ, what a goddamned mess. You turn away.

Finally, next comes your fire. It's the same old noise from the news last night. Nothing new you didn't already know. No suspects, no witnesses, five crispy critters they're calling victims. Next.

You are kind of relieved but you are kind of miffed too. Bumped for an overturned truck full of pigs. That's bullshit. You are much more happening than dead pigs blocking traffic by the airport. What the hell are those news people thinking? You suppose if that dog had crawled back into that drainpipe again today, you'd have been bumped back even further.

There is a knock at the door and you open it. It's Dan and he is pissed.

"Fuckin' pigs. Do you believe that shit? Motherfuckin', goddamned pigs for Christ's sake."

He grins as wide as a house. It is pretty funny when you think about it.

The phone rings and you know who it has to be.

"Fucking pigs. Do you believe it?" Nikko says on the other end. "See you in a couple of minutes."

You hang up the phone and turn to Hale and Dan.

"Hey, that was Bo's agent. Paramount wants him to read for *Weekend at Bernies 3*."

"Bullshit," Dan says.

You give him a look he's seen from you at least a million times before. It's the raised eyebrow and squinty eyed *you must have just become mentally challenged* look.

"What?" he asks. It's short for *What the hell is wrong with you?*

"You probably still think Tupak Shakur is some kind of Jewish holiday, don't you?" Hale says, grinning. Man, do you love ribbing Dan when the chance arrives, which is often.

"Fuck both of you. I mean it." Dan folds his arms.

You laugh pretty hard and so does Hale. Dan knows it's all at his expense so he doesn't join you. There is a knock at the door and you figure Nikko must have ran all the way over to get here this fast. You open your yap at the same time you open the door.

"Hey killer," you say, catching yourself way too late. It isn't Nikko.

"Killer? Hey man, I don't even eat meat," says Mooch. He's looking at you kind of funny.

"Sorry man, in this light you kind of look like a young Jerry Lee Lewis," you tell him. You look over at Hale and he just kind of shrugs. Mooch looks more like Jerry Lewis, a red haired, Irish Nutty Professor.

"Hey, dudes, they're showing *The Wall* and *Heavy Metal* back to back at Willington tonight. Some of us are going to shroom and go," Mooch says.

Willington Pavilion is a student center on the far side of campus and on weekend nights they usually show old movies for free. You and Jackie went a lot since neither of you really had much money to go out and do real stuff in the real world. Without a doubt it was always a pretty decent time and a good place to score some dope if you were looking. If you didn't have your terrorist's round table tonight with the boys you'd commit to going, although the thought of trying to watch *The Wall* on hallucinogens seems more frightening than exciting.

"Maybe we'll catch up with you later," says Hale. "We're trying to plan a surprise party for Nikko."

"Right on," replies Mooch. "Catch ya later."

"Later," you say

"Ad-yoze," he says, shooting you a peace sign in the process. You shut the door behind him.

You jerk your thumb at the door. "A *right on* and a peace sign," you tell Hale. "That kid needs to go down to Long Beach and let some dockworkers kick the shit out of him for a while."

"Dude, that wasn't a peace sign," Hale tells you. "That was a 'V' for Vicodin." He is probably right. All you ever did was smoke a little weed. You look like mamma's boys next to Mooch and his roommate. Those guys have dropped acid more times than you've dropped your pants and yet they still manage to keep their grade point averages above Hale's. It bugged him to no end. The Moocher did so much dope he made Woodstock look like an old ladies tea social and he still pulled a three point four.

"I think I got a contact high from him just stopping by," says Hale.

Dan laughs and there is another knock at the door. You open it and it's Nikko this time.

"Hey killer," he says, walking past you to your desk.

THE DOOMSDAY CLUB   89

"Killer?" you say to him. "Hey man, I don't even beat my meat."

Nikko doesn't get it but Hale and Dan are laughing hysterically. You don't think it was that funny. Perhaps it was your delivery.

"Allow me to explain what will be the most exciting moment yet of your pathetic drug addled lives," Nikko kids. He reaches into his bag and pulls out some sketches. What a motivated little terrorist bastard he is. There are quick line drawings of the street, of the layout of Chicky's and the bathroom. He spent the better part of the afternoon storyboarding your bomb scare. You are impressed.

"Quite simple gentlemen," he proceeds. "The bathroom is between the restaurant and the bagel shop. Hale goes in with Scott."

"Why me?" you interrupt. You were hoping for an easy task in this whole boondoggle.

"Because you know the layout," Nikko says, impatiently. "Hale goes in and watches the door while Scott sets the detonator and dumps the carbide. You slap an *out of order* sign on the door and crazy glue the lock so that no one can open it. Bam. You're out in sixty seconds."

"Whoever gets the key is going to be seen by the security camera in Chicky's."

"Don't need it." Nikko produces a key-shaped replica. You take it from him and examine it closely. It's plastic.

"Lucite," Nikko continues. "I traced the outline of the key onto a paper towel when I was in the can with it. I used it to make a dupe at my lab with a diamond headed cutting tool."

You knew it. You really can find all the stuff you need to blow up anything at almost any college. You just have to know where to look or who to ask.

"So what the fuck do I do then?" asks Dan.

"Well, one of you guys has to drive. I think it should be Hale since his car is less conspicuous," Nikko says. He is right. A black Camry would blend in a lot better in Beverly Hills than a beat up white Chevy pickup. "That means Dan, you have to make the phone call to report it."

"Not to 911," Hale says. "They'll record his voice. They record all of their calls." A-ha. Now you're positive he's been watching *CSI*.

"How about a radio station?" you ask.

"I was thinking a newspaper but a radio station would be better," Nikko says.

"Just not the college station," Hale adds. "That'd be way too obvious."

"Agreed," says Nikko.

"And whatever you do, don't call from your own phone. Radio stations have caller I.D. now to screen for cranks," says Hale. "Besides, the cops could find it if they run the MUD's."

"MUD's?"

"Message Unit Detail reports. Those are the records of every call that any phone receives. You can't get that information yourself but if the government wants to know who's been calling you they just check your MUD's."

You look at Hale. Fucking poser.

"What the fuck do I say?" Dan asks.

"I got it," you tell him. You put on your best deep and breathy voice. "There is a bomb at the Chicky's in Beverly Hills like the one that killed the people in the slum building early Thursday morning."

"Add some crap about man being evil," Hale interjects. "You know. The whole apocalypse thing."

You go back to the voice. "Mankind is evil and will be punished by an angry God."

"As Nostradamus has foretold," adds Nikko, jumping in with his own fake deep voice.

"Until you change your wrongful ways," you continue. "I, uh, I mean, The Doomsday Club will continue to cleanse the earth by fire. You have one hour to disarm the bomb."

"Thank you, drive through," jokes Hale.

"Wow, Scott," Nikko says, slapping you on the back. "James Earl Jones doesn't have shit on you."

"Yeah, yeah, yeah," says Dan sarcastically. "I laughed, I cried, it was better than *Cats*. Now which one of you fuckers is going to write that all down for me?"

ONE0

For some reason it hits you as a surprise that Nikko wants to go and do it right now. You really don't feel prepared for some reason. It's not like you need any advance notice to be ready, you just feel uncomfortable since don't have any time to even think about chickening out. Not that you would, of course, but you'd at least like the chance to consider it. Everybody knows it too. Hey, come on, it's all fun and games when it's all just talk.

To some extent, it seems ridiculous to put yourselves this much in danger of being caught planting another bomb right now. Actually, it seems pretty fucking stupid. There isn't any heat on you yet but with the possibility that someone might have seen something, you have no idea if there's any coming. It seems extremely brain dead though to wait until the police are knocking on your door wanting to ask you a few questions. Doing this is a pre-emptive strike on your part—to send the cops looking in the wrong direction. You have to keep reminding yourself of that.

There's no doubt about it. You have kind of screwed the pooch big time and now it's starting to snowball. In your madness you believe that it is still manageable if you take matters into your own hands. It is inevitable there'll be police around here in the next day or two investigating Bo's vanishing act. That is a given. Since no one will probably ever I.D. his ashes, you just want to make certain the cops never think of the five bodies in the fire and his disappearance to be anything more than unrelated events in a city where people get killed and others vanish every day.

This is a simple gag. In, out, nobody gets hurt and the end

result is the cops get a vapor trail to chase. A new clue they can chew on for a while that won't mean shit in the long run. What the hell? You don't have anything else better to do tonight anyway and the sooner this is all over, the sooner you can get your personal comeback on track. You can't shake the need for some weed right now. Though it might make you less nervous, it might just make you paranoid instead and this isn't the time or place for that.

Pulling the Banana Republic bag out of the closet, you dump the shirt out onto your bed. You hand the bag to Nikko to put his bomb stuff in. You pull a blank sheet of paper out of your desk drawer and quickly make a sign that says *Out of order* and underneath that, *Use ladies room*. Hale hands you some masking tape and you toss both into the bag. The shopping bag is much less conspicuous than a knapsack would be, especially in the area around Rodeo. Although you don't say anything to anybody, you feel getting the bag this afternoon is brilliant on your part. If you could only be this damn smart when it came to school stuff or women for that matter.

Nikko grabs his knapsack too and you head out in Hale's Camry. You can tell he hardly ever uses the car because it's so clean inside. Yours has all kinds of shit in it like maps, old valet parking stubs and soda cans. Hale's car is nearly showroom clean. You ride shotgun and Nikko perches in the back with the bag on the floor between his legs. You catch the faint odor of new car which is one goddamned smell you can't stand so you crack open your window a little bit.

It is six-fifteen and the usual rush hour crush has lessened but the traffic is still messy. Your drive with Nikko this afternoon took just about twenty-five minutes each way. Tonight it's going to take at least twice as long if not longer.

You wrote down everything Dan was supposed to say on a piece of paper and gave him a list of radio stations to get numbers for. It really didn't matter which one he called but Hale told him to pass on the Spanish language ones or he'd be pulling his hair out. His job wasn't as easy as it sounded. By making the call he was exposing himself to getting caught much more than you. You were trying to remember if anybody had said anything to him about being careful about not being seen by anybody and wiping his prints off of the phone and all that stuff. You're sure somebody did but you also feel things were getting a bit sloppy, too. If all went as planned you'd be on your way back to school in just about one hour and Dan would make the call thirty minutes after that.

In the car, you go over the plan again as you creep along in traffic and this time you keep from singing because there's no use in annoying the cat with the bomb. You check your watch and wonder why you don't really feel anything yet. Not excitement, not fear, not boredom or hunger or joy or sorrow. Nothing, not a single solitary thing.

Part of your brain tries to convince the rest of you that it's just calm you are feeling but that isn't really working all that well. Although you don't want to call it panic, what you are feeling is the exact opposite of calm. It's as if your cerebral cortex has shut down entirely, like if you fried a circuit and your body isn't accepting any new input whatsoever. So sorry, this just won't compute, please try again later. 404 error. You've reached a page that doesn't exist. You watch the other cars roll by and just stare out the window. Hale is talking to Nikko but you pay no attention.

Your thoughts turn to Amanda. How come you never noticed her before? Or had you? She was an incredibly good looking girl and you have no idea how you could be living in the same building, shit, on the same floor, and not notice her. Were you slipping? You know you had to have talked to each other before the fire drill. At a party? In the TV lounge? That wasn't it. You are pretty sure that you know her from somewhere. Maybe she came to the home games? She didn't seem like the type. You liked her and she was very sexy, but was it too soon after Jackie to really know what you were feeling? Did it even matter? You were feeling something other than the loathsome weight of the shackles of self-pity and that's what counted on the big tote board. Score one for Scott, down but not out and dangerously close to being able to get his shit together again.

Hale shakes your shoulder.

"Scott. Hey, ground control to Major Scott."

"Huh?"

"What time do you have?" he asks. The clock on his dashboard says it's two-thirty-nine, which is most definitely wrong. You are spacing again. This is certainly not the time for it. You have to put on your gameface and try to focus.

"Almost seven," you tell him.

"Dan should be on his way about now," Nikko says.

He is right. Dan should be on his way, in his pickup heading north to find a pay phone as far away from school as he could get in forty five minutes. The problem is that Dan isn't going anywhere just yet. Little do any of you even know, Dan is stuck in traffic. Not like the stop and go that you are in. The 405 freeway headed north has become a parking lot. That's where he is, sitting motionless in a giant sea of pissed off commuters.

The interchange to the 101 is blocked because of an accident that has traffic slammed for miles. In Southern California, you get about three-hundred gorgeous and sunny days, perfect days. Half of what's left is rainy and shitty and the other half is somewhere in between. It is still what they call the rainy season which means brief showers once or twice a week at most. Snow in L.A. would be the seventh sign of the Apocalypse, you are sure about it.

As the weather report had predicted, a brief shower had washed through momentarily and although it slowed traffic down slightly, everybody on their afternoon commute was dealing with it rather well. Except, that is, for one person. A construction worker on his way home after stopping for a couple of brews with the boys tried in vain to not miss his exit by cutting off a minivan. The minivan wouldn't let him in so the construction worker sped up and ended up hydroplaning on the newly slicked highway into a retaining wall and bouncing back into traffic. The minivan sped away without a scratch but the less-than-sober construction worker hit two other cars. A half an hour later the police were able to open up one of the four northbound lanes. No one was hurt too seriously but there would be a lot of overcooked dinners on the family table tonight.

Dan doesn't have a single clue as to what is going on because, like most of the interior gadgets in his truck, the radio doesn't work and he never bothered to fix it. He is gridlocked in on all sides and not moving, sweating bullets like a madman sitting there with no way to get in touch with you. On a team, nobody wants to be the guy that screws it all up and, right now, Dan is facing the prospect of dropping the ball when it really counts. A real shit deal that nobody wants on their permanent record.

"Fuck me!" he screams, slamming the palm of his hand against the steering wheel.

Hale makes the turn off of Sunset onto Beverly and your heart is racing. Once you get close, you finally start to feel the slight onset of the rush again and it's making you nervous. After seven, most of the stores have closed but there are still a lot of people out and about, sticking their faces in windows up and down the street. You look at the scurrying pedestrians on their way to wherever and wonder if anyone would even notice you. People here are wonderful at ignoring other folks in general so maybe you'll be like ghosts in the shadows. It isn't like a city vibe where people minded their own business; it's just that out here people spend so much time making sure you notice them that they hardly notice you in return. You make a point of remembering to keep your head down and to avoid eye contact if possible. You just have to play it cool and follow Nikko's lead. He is nervous too, you can tell.

He pulls his bottle of Evian from his knapsack and pours off some of it into the detonator while you are still in the car. You're glad he thought to do this now instead of when you were sitting there like ducks in the can. There is no way you are going to stand out there for one second more than you have to. You don't think you could take it.

After pausing for a moment he pulls some more beans from his bag and adds them to the jar. Maybe it's all your imagination but there is something bothering you about the detonator, about the way it looks. Nikko's jar of magic beans looks different for some reason. You let the thought pass, the detonator will take care of itself, right? You have to make sure you don't get caught. Although never spoken, getting arrested would be like being handed a free ass-whipping coupon redeemable at your parents house, along with a get-out-of-your-future-free card redeemable at the county courthouse. Being the lookout makes your palms sweat furiously, but you can't deny something about it is also very exciting.

You shoot Nikko a look and he just holds up a hand and nods and keeps checking the jar. You are sure he knows what he's doing. Damn, you are praying he does but you can tell that your balls aren't completely convinced at all. He screws the cap onto the detonator and you watch nervously as he wipes it down. He takes a slug off of the water bottle and offers it to you and all of a sudden you become aware of how much your mouth feels like someone has lined it with burlap. Your pulse has picked up considerably in the last few seconds as you fidget in your seat like your pants have been set on fire.

There are drivers looking for metered parking but it is obvious that there is none to be found anywhere so you roll slowly by Chicky's. You look out the window and it appears like the dinner crowd at this hour is light, actually a little lighter than you thought it would be just a moment ago. The Bagelry looks closed. This is as good as it's going to get.

Unbeknownst to you, Dan looks at his watch for the fifth time in the last five minutes. It says seven-twenty but he knows it's most likely wrong. Like the truck, it ran good enough for the present and he always figured he'd worry about replacing it after graduation.

That's if they let you graduate from jail, a little voice in his head was telling him. Oddly enough, he thought, the little voice always sounded too much like his mother.

"Fuck!" he screams again. It's been over ten minutes since he last moved at all. The traffic is at a complete standstill. He can see the tops of the cars in the southbound lanes gliding along normally but in front of him is a sea of red brake lights. After all these years, he should have known that something like this could happen. Getting stuck on the freeway is just a way of life out here like heat in Miami or incest in West Virginia.

"Fuck! Fuck! Fuck!" he yells, each time slamming his fist into the roof of his truck. Nobody seems to notice though because this is a perfectly normal reaction to have in L.A. traffic.

Hale takes a right at the end of the block and pulls over in front of a hydrant so you can jump out. His job is to just go down a couple of blocks, circle around and get you in a few minutes, and if he doesn't see you, to do it again. If for some reason you aren't there on his second trip around he is to just leave without you. You don't think this is necessary, but Nikko insists on it. Worst case scenario, if anything happens, you all make some sort of half-assed run for it. It seems so melodramatic. You think for a second he might even have a cyanide capsule to swallow if you got caught. The little jerk probably only brought one, too.

Nikko carries the Banana Republic bag carefully. You keep reminding yourself why you are doing this in the first place. After this gag you are retired from the phony terrorist business, free to get on with your life regardless of how banal and pathetic it may seem sometimes. Someday, you're sure you'll be sitting around a table with a pitcher of Coors, having a good laugh over all of this. Yucking it up over the junkies and jarheads you burned up. You can hardly wait. It sounds about as much fun as a body cavity search performed by Captain Hook.

It's only a half a block to Chicky's and you walk casually, almost stroll, like a couple of guys in no rush to go anywhere. Nothing can be further from the truth. You feel short of breath and weak-kneed and you just want to do the deed and get going.

You walk down Beverly nice and slow like you haven't a care in the whole wide world. If the detonator tips over, the bag might get wet and that, although seemingly insignificant, may be something some potential witness remembers. A woman jogs by in sweats and an older couple strolls past not even noticing you. You are as innocuous as possible, blending in perfectly.

A tall, dark-haired guy comes out of Chicky's carrying some take-out and goes to unlock his bike from a no parking sign ten feet away from you. For a moment you think you recognize him as some Shemp you had Freshman Drafting with. Just your luck, the whole thing blown because you bump into somebody you spoke six words to four years ago. You are ready to call the whole thing off. If you are recognized you'll have to bail but then you realize there's no way to get hold of Dan. Bastard doesn't have a cell phone. Your heart feels like it is pounding in your neck. Your shit luck is catching up to you again.

Dark Hair turns his head to the side and you let loose a heavy sigh. It isn't anybody you know. Your mind is playing tricks. This isn't good at all. You have to keep it together. The excitement and nervousness makes you edgy and you just want to take a big time out so you can smoke some weed and shake these jitters.

Just think how easy this would have been at Mardi Gras, the little evil voice in you says. It was right. There you could walk around with a mask on and everyone was shitfaced anyway. It would be way too easy compared to this.

In front of the Bagelry you look out from the corner of your eye. You spot a handful of yuppie customers inside Chicky's but nobody pays any attention to you. You are any two dudes just walking down the street who just happen to be carrying a bag loaded up with fiery death. No biggie. Nikko opens the door between the two stores that leads into the hallway where the bathrooms are and you go in.

Gently dropping the bag on the floor, Nikko pulls out two sets of rubber doctor's gloves from his pocket and hands you a pair. You both put them on. You rub your fingers together nervously listening to the sound of latex against latex as you stare at the men's room door. It's showtime.

Nikko pulls the lucite key out of his pocket when you both hear something. There is no mistaking what it is either, no mistaking it at all. It's a sound you would have recognized even if you were six years old. Someone is taking a shit in the men's room.

Traffic has finally started to move on the freeway again, slowly for sure, but it is moving. Dan's knuckles are turning white. He knows he has less than twenty minutes to get as far away as possible and that it isn't going to be enough. When he got in the truck at five before seven he had zeroed the odometer and now it reads five point one miles.

"I could have fuckin' walked that far in this time," he says out loud to himself. "With a limp *and* a log tied to my ass."

Two minutes later he gets clear of the tangle. As he passes the pileup he looks over at the construction worker's Caprice and shoots it the finger.

"Serves you right, fuckin' jerk!" he screams. His windows are rolled up and nobody hears him but it makes Dan feel a bit better to vent. He looks at his watch again. It is almost seven-thirty. The ball is definitely dropping from his fingers.

There are little white half-moons your nails have made in your glove from clenching your fists so tight. For a second, you are afraid you may have ripped them but you haven't. Nikko is biting his lip. You look at him and shake your head. You point to the door.

"That guy's going to see us when he comes out," you whisper.

Nikko hadn't thought about that. His eyes widen like teacups.

Another groan comes from behind the door. Whoever is in there is in the middle of leaving their entire intestines behind.

"I'm going to try the ladies room," he whispers.

You nod, you really don't see much choice. You have been standing here for sixty seconds already and haven't done anything except get closer to getting seen. The hallway is so narrow that when the mystery guest comes out of the bathroom you'll be face to face with him unless you hide in the tiny ladies room. That is *if* he ever does come out of there. You hear the rustling sound of a newspaper page being turned and start to think the guy has moved in. If someone sees you now, it would be entirely suspicious.

Your breathing is fast and you are afraid of hyperventilating and passing the hell out right here on the linoleum floor. You look down at the floor tile. It is black and white checked and looks like it would feel nice and cool if you rested your cheek against it.

Making floor tile, now that would be a shitty job, you think to yourself. It would sure beat the piss out of stamping license plates and breaking rocks though. Your thoughts are all over the place and you can't concentrate. It is your responsibility to keep watch and all you can do is stare at the floor.

Nikko grabs the doorknob to the ladies room and slips the key into the lock slowly. You can hear each tumbler click into place. He turns the knob and for an instant you think it isn't going to open. His was a copy of the men's room key, it's not going to work. You are sure of it.

It's not going to work, Dan thinks to himself. His original plan, to get to a reststop he knew of way out in Santa Clarita, is fading fast. Even if there weren't any speed traps to avoid, he knows for certain his pickup would never make that kind of ground in the next fifteen minutes. Maybe half that far if he's lucky. He pushes the truck past seventy and the cab bucks like a paint shaker. It occurs to Dan that he is going to have to exit pretty soon and find a phone in the Valley.

You would have bet your bike that Nikko's lucite key wouldn't work, especially not on the ladies room door, but he takes a deep breath and turns the knob. It opens. He winks at you and pokes his head in. You look over your shoulder to see if anyone is coming into the hallway and there is nothing. You are clear. He flips on the light and the whir of a fan comes on with it.

Nikko notices it too. "No..." he whispers. He is looking up at it, jaw agape. "Mother fucker!"

"What?"

"The vent. I forgot to take the vent into account, I'm so fucking stupid!" He points at the standard-issue public toilet vent fan. "The gas will escape."

"It only comes on when you turn on the light switch," you

whisper. "If the lock is broken then no one can come in and hit the switch."

"Yes, but we don't know where that vent goes to. The gas is going to rise up into it and what if it connects somewhere to the kitchen vent from next door," Nikko explains to you. "One spark and this whole place goes boom-boom anytime after the carbide starts turning into acetylene."

Oh shit. You get it. If you really did want to blow this place this would be the way to do it, you wouldn't even need a detonator. Once the gas got into the vent, anything with a flame, an oven or even a cigarette, could potentially set it off anytime. That's not what you had in mind.

"We're done, let's get out of here," he says. You are going to abort the whole thing. Without being able to get a hold of Dan to stop him from making the phone call though you are hosed.

"Wait," you say, grabbing his arm. "Try the mop closet."

Nikko nods. Why the hell wouldn't it work? The key works on both of the bathrooms. His hands are shaking.

You look down the hallway through the glass door that opens onto the sidewalk. People pass by with their bags from Guess or Coach or Bijan or holding hands with their dates but nobody is coming in. From behind the door of the men's room you hear another newspaper page turn. Another grunt. Another splash.

You have been in this hallway for way too long. If this were an hour earlier, you'd have the whole dinner crowd but since it is later you are lucking out big time. Someone else is bound to come in to use the can soon though. It is the mop closet or nothing and it has to be right now.

The lock on the door takes the key like a long lost lover but when Nikko tries the knob, it doesn't turn.

"Jiggle it," you whisper.

He does and you hear the soft click of what sounds like the last tumbler falling into place. The door opens. You'll later wish that it hadn't.

As you had guessed, it's a closet. The shelves are covered with several gallon size plastic jugs of pink and blue colored cleaning solutions, aerosol cans of disinfectant, dozens of rolls of single-ply toilet paper and stacks of paper towels. In the corner are a plunger and a squeegee, and on the wall is a sink. If your job is cleaning the shitter then this is your office. Getting a desk or a chair in here is completely out of the question. You'd be hard pressed to even stand without taking the mop and its rolling bucket out first.

Nikko looks over at the sink. You shake your head and point to the bucket. It looks half-full of a foul, grey colored, dirty liquid you assume is mostly water. The mildewy smell coming out of it makes you think it hasn't been emptied in days. Nikko looks at you and wrinkles his nose.

You wait for him to say something else but he takes the carbide powder out of the bag and dumps it into the bucket. For a second, you watch it fizz like a big dirty glass of seltzer. Nikko checks the detonator one last time. It does look different to you for some reason.

The beans.

The detonator that Nikko used to blow up the slum building had kidney beans in it. This one was full of what looked like lima beans. How much of a difference would that make? Not much, you hope.

At this point though, it doesn't matter. What does, is just finishing up and getting the hell out of here as soon as possible. Nikko holds the jar up to the light and at first you can't tell what he is doing.

"Just put the damn thing in for God's sake!" you whisper.

"I'm making sure there aren't any fingerprints on it."

You have only been in here a few minutes but it feels like a few hours already. Your skin is starting to crawl and you are half afraid what you feel is your skeleton trying to jump free of the rest of you and make a break for it. Not a pretty picture. Either that or you are bound to strangle Nikko just on general principle.

Your train of thought is suddenly derailed by the sound of a toilet flushing.

Nikko looks at you and freezes, still holding the detonator jar up to the light. At best you have a few seconds before the mystery guest comes out and catches you in the act right there at door number three. You can only hope whoever is in there is still sitting there reading Dilbert or checking their horoscope.

Sometimes, your problem is you think too much and it holds you back. It causes you to hesitate and you just stand there like a big buffoon catching flies in your mouth. Other times life becomes akin to that moment when you watch the ball come out of the pitcher's hand and, in that split second before it crosses the plate, you calculate where, when and how hard to swing that bat. It's your brain working on its own, the way it works best without your conscious self getting in the way. It's part reflex reaction, part instinct and a healthy dose of good old-fashioned guesswork mixed with luck. You are about to have that moment right now.

Before you can think twice about anything, you shut the closet door and push the now-startled Nikko into the still-open ladies room. He's about to say something but you clamp your hand over his mouth. This is the second time you've found yourself hiding out in a ladies bathroom in the past three days and it is a habit you'll be willing to give up entirely once this whole episode is over and done with. You can feel your heart pounding again and the blood shooting through your veins. For the moment you are 007, if only in your mind.

It isn't a second too soon either because you can hear the men's room door open and close. Whoever it is, is leaving but not in any big hurry. What sounds like the shuffling of footsteps makes you think it has to be an old guy. The shuffling sound stops and you put your ear against the door and listen as he coughs up what sounds like a large lung nugget before moving on. Your grandfather was like that, always had lots of phlegm and snot after taking a good dump. It was disgusting but if it's gotta come out then it's gotta come out. You hear the outside door open and shut again and finally throw the ladies room door open and peek out. Two guys in the ladies john is suspicious alright, even Bond would have trouble talking his way out of that.

"Jesus!" Nikko waves his hand in front of his face.

He's right, you don't know what gramps had for dinner but you guess it didn't quite agree with him. You are worried about other things though, like your ass. You look over to check that the makeshift key is still in the closet door.

I wonder if the old guy noticed that? you think to yourself.

It doesn't matter now. You grab the detonator out of Nikko's hand, put it on a shelf and entomb it in the closet. The time for subtlety has passed. You have to get the hell out now. You grab the bag and make a move for the outside door. For your next trick, you plan to disappear. Your balls are in complete agreement.

Grabbing your arm, Nikko looks at you and then at the closet door. He is finally unfrozen but not moving.

"Super glue," he whispers, pointing at the doorknob. "The lock."

Damn, damn, damn. The tube of super glue is at the bottom of the bag. Instead, you reach over and grab the head of the lucite key. With one quick jerk of your wrist you snap it in half, leaving most of it in the lock. That will have to do. You grab Nikko and push him down the short hallway to the outside door.

You half-stumble out onto the sidewalk. Out of the corner of your eye, you see that Hale's Camry is passing by at the moment you come out of the door and isn't stopping. He doesn't see you and even if he had, he knows better than to pick you up in front of Chicky's like that. Man, this sucks. Ten seconds earlier and you'd be on your way back to school right now. You and Nikko are going to have to keep walking in the opposite direction and hope to catch him on his next time around the block.

That is if there is a next time. You check your watch. You were only in there for about five minutes, more than enough time even in this traffic for Hale to circle around a few blocks and come back at least twice and that's what you are afraid of. What if he had already decided to take off like he'd been told to? Catching a cab back to school would be like signing your names all over the bomb. You might as well just sit here on the curb and greet the cops when they show up.

Oh man, this isn't happening, you think to yourself.

Nikko doesn't see the Camry pass by and that's just as well. You are having enough of a time keeping your own panic jammed down your throat without having to deal with his too. Keep your eyes straight and keep walking. At the end of the block, you turn left and let out a large sigh. Without even knowing it you've been holding your breath since you hit the street. It makes you feel a bit light headed. Your heart goes thump, and thump, and thump.

"I think we did it," Nikko says to you softly.

"We're not out of the woods yet, Red Riding Hood," you tell him.

You check your watch again. It will be a couple of minutes before Hale comes back around, that is, if he does come back around. For all you know he could be on his way to Mexico.

You don't like that thought one bit and try to keep it out of your head.

"I wish Hale would hurry up," Nikko says.

There's no doubt that you would have agreed but you are too busy clenching your jaw at that moment. You keep walking. If you don't see the Camry in the next two minutes you are going to jump a cab to the airport with or without Nikko. Nestled in your wallet is your emergency Visa card, and if this doesn't qualify then your mom and stepdad can kiss your ass.

You are too busy actually looking to see if there are any cabs around when Nikko spots the Camry.

"There." He points.

Hale sees you and shoots a little *let's get the fuck out of Dodge* kind of wave your way. He pulls over and you both get in quickly. The door handle feels funny to you and you realize you are still wearing the latex gloves on your hands. Did anyone see that? Two guys walking through downtown Beverly Hills with rubber gloves on. It doesn't matter now.

The rush comes as soon as you shut the door and Hale pulls away from the curb. It starts at your head and you can imagine what a volcano must feel like, but completely in reverse. You feel almost limp as it washes over you like a big wave crashing onto your head. This is definitely bigger than the one from the last bomb or even bigger than the one you got from killing Bo. It is as if you have come a thousand times in the space of seconds. You feel drained. You are going to get away with it. In an instant you realize it doesn't matter why you've put the bomb there, all that matters is that you again have pissed in the face of danger and won.

"I almost thought you guys got caught or something." Hale seems short of breath.

Pulling your rubber gloves off, you shoot him the Dan hand sign.

"Fucking A!" Nikko yells from the backseat, slapping you on the back at the same time. You head back to school, hoping Dan hasn't mucked up his part of the game plan.

ONEONE

Van Nuys looks shitty. Not like South Central or Inglewood shitty and dangerous—more like strip malls, gas stations and fast food joints endlessly dotting the landscape for miles on end shitty and soulless. Dan knew about this area. Not enough to help him find an isolated pay phone though.

Not that there aren't plenty of places to call from, there are phones everywhere. There is one at every corner and probably one in every store and restaurant and doghouse for miles which just went to show you that what the Valley lacks in character it certainly makes up for in public phones. And donut shops. Lots and lots of donut shops.

Dan pulls off Sepulveda into the parking lot of a 7-Eleven and up to a space by the door. There's a pay phone attached to the side of the building, though he isn't too terribly interested in this one. He looks into his rear view mirror again. The phone he wants is across the street in front of the Amoco.

He checks his watch again. Then takes out the script you've made for him. Across the top, you've written in all caps—

READ SLOW.

Hale had suggested that he read it with a phony accent too. Nikko wanted Dan to do it with a southern drawl. Hale nixed the idea fearing you'd appear to be some hillbilly militia instead of world class terrorists. God forbid someone thought of you as the cruddy domestic kind.

You thought maybe a proper British accent would be the funniest. Professor Henry Higgins, terrorist. The bomb in the john is mainly just a con.

"Just do it in your own accent," Hale finally said, laughing.

"What are you talking about?" Dan replied. "I don't have any fuckin' accent."

That's the way you left it. Dan was just going to read it slow and clear and then get off the phone and drive back. Plain and simple. He reads through the script one more time and turns the page over to make sure he has written down the phone numbers of those radio stations.

He goes into the store to break a twenty and the clerk gives him a dollar in change with his smokes. He takes one last drag on a cigarette, crushes it in the half-full ashtray and gets out of his truck and crosses the street. It's a couple of minutes early but, sitting around and waiting was making him even more nervous than being in traffic. Besides, he had drawn the shit detail of the evening and all because Hale had a nicer car.

"Fuck those guys," he mutters. "The next time they need to haul a stiff away they can put him in the front seat of Hale's Camry and go use the carpool lane."

The reason radio is considered a medium in L.A. is because it's neither rare nor well done. The FM dial is crammed with some thirty-odd stations, half of them Spanish. One of the things you learned on your drive across country was, nine times out of ten, your chances of getting anything worth a shit on the radio were slim to no-fucking-way. One day when you had just crossed the

Rockies all you could pick up was country music and radio evangelists for eight whole hours. It was complete torture. You ended up listening over and over and over to a Cardigans CD Jackie had left in your glove box until you finally tossed it right out of the goddamned window. It wasn't until you hit the ocean that you finally found a station that played anything resembling AOR again.

In town there were, at best, a handful of listenable radio stations to pop back and forth to. Usually you could only go so long before somebody would go and play something shitty like Rob Thomas or Hot Hot Heat and you'd just hit another preset on your stereo. Hands down, the best station in town was KLXA who usually played the least amount of garbage and the DJ's kept the chatter to a minimum. Since their phone number was 949-KLXA it was easy to remember. That's who Dan decided to call.

You didn't think that it mattered one bit which part of the radio station he called, so you told him to try the request line. You figured there would always be someone answering that phone. If you had known what was going to happen next you would have told him to call a newspaper instead. Look, you're no genius.

He drops a quarter and a dime into the phone and watches his hand shake as he punches in the number. In his other hand he holds the script and glances over his shoulder to see if anyone is watching him. It starts to ring on the other end.

After the second ring, a sedan pulls into the Amoco station. Dan thinks it might be a police car and gets all spooked before hanging up the phone. The guy in the car pulls up to the cashier's booth, gets out to buy a pack of smokes and pulls away. The car is a Chevy Cavalier, which is only marginally more believable as a cop car than a Neon. Dan is getting scared for no reason. He watches until the Cavalier leaves before pulling his money out of the coin return to try again.

"Be cool," he reminds himself. He punches the number in again and listens to it start to ring.

Three rings and nobody is picking up. Dan shakes his head, thinking he'll have to try one of the other stations in town when all of a sudden there is a click on the other end. Before Dan can say anything he hears the DJ's voice blasting into his ear.

"Hey, you're the fifteenth caller! You just won a pair of Green Day tickets!"

"Oh my God!" he yells. "I can't believe it!" Dan is in shock. The bastard is ecstatic.

Green Day had been sold out for months already. You and Dan wanted to go and you found a scalper with decent seats who'd sell them for two hundred bucks apiece. You didn't have that kind of scratch to spend, not on Green Day anyway.

"Who's this?" the DJ thunders.

"Uh, Dan."

"Hey, Dan, hang on and we'll talk to you on the air after this song," the DJ says and before Dan can get in another word, he is on hold.

Oh shit! he thinks to himself. The call. The goddamn bomb call. The whole gig. He looks at his watch. It was ten to eight, five minutes behind schedule. But Green Fuckin' Day tickets? Christ, how often does that happen? What luck.

"I can wait," Dan thinks. "I can wait."

You would think that most people would stick around to see their prank go down but you, Hale and Nikko want to be as far away from Beverly Hills as possible when the shit came down. When the cops roll up and the bomb squad arrives, you want to be back at the room sucking dope into your lungs. You are too busy whooping it up in the car, practically breaking your own arms patting yourselves on the back thinking you are geniuses. You think it's over, that you have pulled it off. If all goes right, you are just going to kick back and watch it all go down on the news at ten.

Man plans and God laughs, remember?

Dan listens to the hold music which is what they are playing on air. The song has just started. *It's okay*, he thinks. The call can wait a couple more minutes.

The DJ comes back on the line five minutes later.

"Well everybody, I have our winner, Dan, on the line. Hey buddy, what's your last name?"

You know things are going to be all fucked up the moment you hear Dan's voice on the radio.

"Wait a second, shut up. That's Dan!" you yell.

"What the fuck is that idiot doing?" Nikko screams from the back seat. No doubt about it. God is laughing alright. He's just plain pissing himself.

"Does that mean he did or didn't make the call?" asks Hale.

It's a good question. How the hell are you supposed to know?

"Dan, where are you calling from?"

Hell, Dan thinks.

"The Valley," Dan says.

"Well, Dan Durden, you just won yourself a pair of Green Day tickets for the show next weekend at the Staples Center. What do you think about that?"

"Uh," Dan says. "Fuh... I mean, uh, cool."

"Great, hold on Dan and we'll get you those tickets," the D.J. announces to all of Los Angeles. "After this break, ten in a row."

Click, Dan is back on hold.

"Shit!" Dan yells into the phone.

"Shit!" screams Hale. "Does that mean he did or didn't call in the bomb?" You look at him. The veneer is cracked slightly. He is definitely losing his cool.

"I don't know!" yells Nikko. "I, oh, uh...FUCK!" He slams his hand on the back of your seat. This is a first. You are the prevailing head of cool for once.

"Okay, wait, think about it," you tell them. "He calls in a bomb and to congratulate him they put him on the air and give him concert tickets?"

"Scott's right. No way," says Hale. He points at the clock on the Camry's dash. "It's almost eight, he must have called the threat in before."

"Yeah, but what phone did he use to win the tickets?" asks Nikko.

He is only on hold for another minute but it's long enough for Dan to realize the most important thing about what happened by the time he hung up.

He couldn't use this phone again.

The police would be able to locate the source of the bomb threat call because eventually they'd access all those MUD's that Hale had mentioned. If they saw that another call was made to another radio station from the same phone just minutes before they'll know it was the same guy. Dan had just given KLXA and a million of its listeners his full name. Calling from this phone now would be as stupid as calling from the one back in his room. He stuffed the paper into his pocket and ran for his truck.

Not only could he not call from that phone but he was pretty damn sure that calling from that neighborhood was out as well, and now was surely not the time to be playing this whole thing open-assed. His watch says it's eight o'clock and he jumps back onto the freeway, leaving a patch of rubber as his tires screech on the asphalt.

The speed limit is sixty-five and Dan isn't so much afraid of getting pulled over for speeding as he is that his truck is going to fall apart. He is barely pushing seventy-five and the truck is shaking the fillings out of his teeth.

"The next time I need to call in a terrorist threat," Dan says to himself. "I'll fuckin' borrow Scott's car."

He passes an exit for the 118 Freeway and keeps going, cursing the sputtering, clanking sound his engine is starting to make. His foot stays on the floor. He looks around. The truck had to hold together.

"You hear me baby, hold together."

Up ahead he merges onto the 5. It's not too terribly far from Van Nuys but he knows he'll have to call really soon.

"Next exit," Dan mutters. It was almost quarter after.

The Rebel Truck Stop is visible even before the offramp. This will have to do. A beat to shit white Chevy pickup truck isn't going to attract attention in a place like this.

Dan is frantically looking for phone booths. There had to be pay phones in the diner behind the gas station but a phone out in the open like that was unusable for this kind of call. An eighteen-wheeler pulls away from the diesel island and he sees what he's looking for on the back end of the lot.

Three phone booths are standing behind the greasy spoon next to a pair of weather beaten soda machines. In the first one, a rail-thin trucker in a hat picks his nails while talking to someone, but the other two are empty.

I wish Skinny's dime would just run out and he'd paddle his fuckin' ass back onto the highway, Dan thinks. It would be best if there wasn't anybody around at all but he can't wait one more second. This is going to have to do.

He pulls the pickup in front of the booth farthest from Skinny, hoping the phone is working. The last thing Dan wants is to make the call from the booth next to the trucker.

Sliding the door shut behind him, Dan steals a glance back to the other booth. Skinny is still jawing away and paying more attention to his greasy nails than to anything around him. Dan takes a second to see if he can hear anything the trucker is saying. He can, though none of it comprehendible, muffled by the layers of plexiglass and steel that separate the two of them. Digging in his pocket, he pulls out some change and the now crumpled piece of paper that he has to read from.

Turning the page over, he picks another station to call. This time choosing KNGW-AM, the all-news station, figuring that unless they were giving away Anderson Cooper tickets it has to be a safe bet. As he drops in thirty-five cents and dials, he wonders if it's entirely possible to get hit by lightning twice. It if happened, it would be on a day like this. Murphy's law has a way of lingering around like a bad dose of the clap.

The line rings once before someone answers.

"There is a bomb in..."

A familiar voice interrupts him with a pre-recorded message.

"Please deposit another fifty cents."

"Fuck!" he yells. He's traveled far enough out of the area that it isn't a local call anymore. Immediately he looks over at Skinny to see if he's attracting any attention. Skinny doesn't notice anything. He has his back to Dan now and he is most likely still checking out his cuticles.

Frantically, Dan feels around in his pockets for more change, digging out two more quarters. The last of his change. If he gets cut off for any reason, he knows he'll have to go into the greasy spoon to get some more.

He slips the quarters into the slot and waits for the two beeps that tell him his call will go through. They come and once again the phone starts ringing. Dan takes a deep breath. Lights. Camera. Action.

"KNGW, all news, all day. How can I help you?"

Now in a town like L.A., it's a pretty safe bet a radio station like this gets its share of prank calls and rambling lunatics. As Dan starts reading your little threat, it takes the receptionist on the other end ten seconds to place this in her mental in-basket.

On the bottom of the page you had written in big letters the last thing he was to say to whomever he gave this message to. The kicker. It was the only question that he was to ask.

"Do you understand?"

"Yu, yu, yes," the receptionist's voice trembles.

Click.

Before the receptionist can even make the call to her boss, Dan wipes his prints off of the phone with his shirt sleeve, jumps back in his truck and pulls away. He shoots one last look over at Skinny. The trucker now has his boot off and is scratching a dirty sock-covered foot, but at no time does he even look in Dan's direction. It's a clean break. Time to blow like the wind.

His hands are shaking badly as he pulls back onto the 5 freeway headed south, checking the rearview every few seconds.

I remembered to wipe my prints off of the phone, right? Yes, he thought. With the exception that he had made the call thirty minutes late, it had all gone pretty smoothly. How much difference was it going to make in the long run? A lot, but that would become the least of your problems.

ONE2

At about the same time Dan takes a long last look at Skinny behind the Rebel Truck Stop, you pull into the Stonehouse parking lot. Nobody has said anything for the last twenty minutes or so and you can tell you aren't the only one checking to see if a certain beat-to-shit, white Chevy pickup is here. Your celebratory mood is gone and so is your rush. What a total gyp. It's like spending all night trying to get a date into bed and having your roommate walk in just as you're about to close the deal.

Part of you feels completely cheated. You worked your ass off for a hit of that adrenaline and didn't even get a chance to enjoy it —to savor it and suck it all in like an infant at its mommy's breast. The rush had become your milk of life, it was your id food and your id was screaming like a fly-covered Ethiopian baby now. Right before you had gotten your mouthful it was snatched away. You are disappointed alright, but a bit of you is pretty pissed about it too. Dependency has become a big part of your life lately, whether it's Jackie or pot or whatever. You had come to lean too heavily on all of the crutches you had set up in your life and now, on top of everything else, you have become an adrenaline junkie as well. You are gone.

The only sane approach to this whole debacle you can think of is to worry about Dan's call after you've had a chance to talk to (and possibly strangle) him. It seems only reasonable and anything else is liable to give your brain a chance to fly off of the handle. Your balls are handling it all very well which you truly consider to be a good sign in the face of everything so far.

Hale parks the Camry and the three of you all pile out. For a moment you just stand there in the parking lot, looking at each other, your heads hanging in silence. To someone just walking by, you probably look like three kids who just lost the big game. The shitty part of it is that it's not too terribly far from the truth.

You feel your blood sugar bottoming out and suddenly realize you haven't eaten anything since lunch. You aren't exactly hungry but you need something soon or you'll start to get lightheaded, and that is no way to be if you suddenly find yourself on the run to a faraway country. The dining hall is closed by now, but you don't want to get in your car and drive out somewhere to get anything because you have to wait for that idiot Dan to find out if he had hosed the whole deal.

You should have grabbed something at Chicky's while you had the chance, a voice in your head tells you. Ha, ha, ha.

"Let's order a pizza, I'm starving," Hale says

"You read my mind," you tell him.

"Amen to that, brother," Nikko adds.

"Order two, I'm sure that Dan's going to be hungry too," you say. They both look at you.

"Yeah," says Hale. "I hope you're right."

The pizzas will take forty-five minutes and Dan is going to show his ass up by then or your dinner is going to be an in-flight meal on your way to Argentina.

You grab the TV remote. Some unfunny show is on but you can't be bothered to change it. Friday nights are incredibly lame anyway so it doesn't matter what channel you have on. It seems to you like every stupid sitcom is about a single parent trying to raise a houseful of kids, or a fat guy with a hot wife. It's bullshit to begin with. Every kid from a single parent household that you knew growing up did a lot of drugs, and these fucking kids on TV didn't even smoke any dope or cigarettes or even chew gum. Every fat guy you knew in real life had a fat wife. *TV is such crap*, you think. No wonder you can't communicate with anyone else if all of your social skills were taught to you by annoying stand-up comics going through the motions each week for a regular paycheck.

You are starting to be afraid you aren't going to be the least bit hungry when the pizza comes. Hale takes care of that though.

"A friend with weed," he says.

"Is a friend indeed."

You take the bong from him and suck back a gigantic hit. You close your eyes and feel it drift down into your lungs, slowly seeping into your body like a spilled drink on an old rug. Nikko sits on the bed and you pass it to him. He's jonesing for a toke as well. Hale smokes last and afterwards pulls another small bud from the baggie of Snatch's weed and sends the bong around for another lap.

You are feeling much better but your mind is still stuck on the big picture. Every couple of minutes or so you look out the window. You can't see the parking lot from here but you'd be able to see Dan's truck, or the pizza guy or the cops for that matter, coming up the road. It is way past the time he should have been back and you don't say anything about it to the other guys. You don't have to.

Hale offers another hit and you shake your head. It's time to heed the call of nature. As you get up, Nikko spots the Chevy pickup speeding down the road in a hurry. You throw the door to the room open and bolt out into the hallway and run out to the parking lot as fast as your stoned feet will carry you.

You tell yourself to be tactful.

"So what the *fuck* happened to you?"

Dan gets out of the truck and looks at all of you. "You, uh, heard?"

"Yeah, we heard. The whole fucking city heard!" you yell. "What the fuck was that all about?"

"Look, I tried to make the call like we planned."

"Tell me you did," Nikko pleads. He is close to having a panic attack. Shit, so are you at that point.

"Yeah, I made the call, don't worry about it. It's just the first time, I ended up winning those fuckin' tickets. How the fuck was I supposed to know? But hey, the tickets, isn't that cool as shit?"

"Fuck the fucking tickets!" you blurt out. Dan is shocked.

"So what did you do?" Hale asks. You all look back and forth at each other.

"I, uh, got out of the Valley and called from a different phone."

"The Valley? I thought you were going to..." you try to say but Dan cuts you off.

"Yeah, yeah, I was, I was. Some fuckin' goofball rolled his car on the 405 and there was all of this traffic and I only got as far as Van Nuys."

"But the real call," Hale asks him. "Where'd you make that from?"

"Some fuckin' truck stop way up on the 5. Look, I was careful. I just called a little bit later because I had to change phones."

"How much later?" you ask. This was serious.

"I don't know. Twenty minutes, a half-hour. Something like that. But it's cool, I made the call." He pulls the crumpled paper out of his pocket and shows it to you. "I made the call and read the whole thing like you said, word for word."

You take the paper from him and reread what you had written over two hours ago. You relax, thinking it's going to be okay. That is until your eyes catch the next to last sentence.

"You told them they had an hour to disarm the bomb?" you ask. Your balls already know the answer to this one.

"Yeah, that's what it says, right?"

This is bad. You are standing in the tunnel watching the light get bigger and bigger as it comes right at you.

"Even though you called twenty minutes late?"

What you are getting at finally hits everybody else. Nikko tilts his head back and stares at the sky.

"It might have been thirty or forty minutes late," Dan says sheepishly as he starts to look at his shoes.

You look over at Hale and he just shakes his head and laughs. You turn to Nikko and ask. "Is this going to make much of a difference?"

At eight-fifteen, the receptionist who took the call tried to reach the station manager for five minutes before she finally got through to him at home. By the time she told him what had happened and he figured out what to do about it, it was almost eight-thirty. He told her to wait a couple of minutes so he could get a reporter on the scene and then add the time it actually took for her to call 911 and it was already less than ten minutes until the bomb was supposed to go.

Nikko figured he had fixed the detonator to go two hours after you had set it just to be safe. He did it that way to give the police plenty of time to find it and because he couldn't be exact with a timing mechanism made out of beans. He changed from the kidney beans to the lima beans after reading somewhere about their slower absorption rate.

Lesson number one: Don't believe everything you read. The beans were expanding so fast that there wasn't any safety time. It was going to blow at quarter of nine just like you originally wanted everyone to believe.

By seven o'clock all of the stores on Rodeo were closing and the crowd moved over to Beverly Drive where mostly everything stayed open an hour later. Chicky's, however, stayed open until nine on Fridays. Most of the shoppers had all but drifted away but after eight they did a good business with the different tour bus crowds. Drivers knew that their load of passengers would be hungry from all of that expensive shopping so they'd pull up in front of Chicky's and the weary tourists would pile out to buy sandwiches. Any driver who brought in customers was assured a free meal and coffee so it was a popular stop before heading out onto the highway or back to the hotel.

A cross-country charter tour full of rowdy Germans is finishing up their late supper and proudly showing off their purchases, sharing the same stories of shopping on glamour street they were planning to bore their friends and relatives with back home in Munich. When the police car pulls up, all lights and siren, they crane their necks to see what is happening. When the policemen come in and tell everyone they have to get back on their tour bus for their own safety, they start to gather up their things and oblige. Had the cops shown up five minutes earlier they may have gotten everyone out in time.

As one officer helps the retirees out of Chicky's, answering whatever questions he can understand in their broken english without causing a chain reaction of heart murmurs, the other officer grabs the manager and goes to look for the bomb. As the manager suspects, they checked the men's room and find nothing and then the ladies room and find nothing.

Much to the cop's annoyance though, the manager turns out to be a prissy little emotional man. When he is told they have to get all of the customers out of the restaurant, he becomes angry. When the cop pulls him aside to explain why, he becomes anxious. While going along to look in the men's room for a bomb, he becomes afraid and when they find nothing he is at first relieved, then embarrassed. You see, the bathrooms are a mess and when he thinks of the punk kids who must have broken the lock to his mop closet he becomes angry again. When the cop seems very concerned with this and they both realize what must be locked behind that door he becomes scared again and then briefly ashamed as he suddenly realizes he is taking a shit in his pants. That, however lasts no more than a brief second, replaced by a fleeting glint of sudden and extreme surprise at the moment they are both engulfed by the giant fireball.

ONE3

You demolish both pizzas in about ten minutes. The munchies have hit alright and you are as ravenous as a pack of wild dogs when the delivery guy finally rolls up. Fuckin' Dan can't wait long enough and burns the roof of his mouth on the first bite. It doesn't seem to slow him down a bit, or any of you for that matter. You risk the loss of a digit by sticking your hand into the fray to grab yourself another slice.

You suggest afterwards that you boogie down to Willington and catch *Heavy Metal*. The back half of the double feature usually hit at ten so you have a half hour before it starts. Time enough for a quick toke.

Hale left the TV on but has it on mute. You aren't really watching it so it functions more like an electronic fish bowl. The stereo is up and KLOS is playing some Von Bondies (thank fucking Christ) so you lean over and turn it up. Nobody seems to be in any sort of rush to get out of here and it hits you. You have to stick around to watch the news. You completely forgot about your bomb scare. The most fucked up event of the last twenty-four hours and it has slipped your mind like an uncle's wedding anniversary. The dope is definitely taking its toll on your short term memory. Pretty soon you'll have to start writing your name in your underwear.

Everybody wants to stick around and watch your prank on the evening news. You agree, but to be honest, you are getting sick of the whole thing. It's done and you aren't too sure if you even want to hear about it anymore. You'll stick around and watch the news anyway.

Grabbing the remote, you flip around the dial to try and find the Kings' game. On channel 9 they show the Fanta commercial with the girl you're completely in love with. To you, that stuff tastes like turpentine, but there is something about the way this chick chugs it. Your deepest sick fantasy has become you turning into that bottle. You know it's kind of weak, but before this week you thought that smoking a joint in a park was living life on the edge.

Your finger is on the channel-up button, ready to make the jump when the station cuts to a breaking news bulletin. Even as you watch it for a couple of seconds you don't even realize what it is. You absently flip to another channel when Hale grabs the remote out of your hands.

"Whoa, shit!" he yells.

It takes a second before he can get the sound back on but once you realize the blazing fire you are seeing is Chicky's there is no mistaking what must have happened.

You look over and Nikko and Dan looks at both of you. His mouth is open so wide you could stuff a melon into it.

"What the fuck did you guys do?"

What did we do? Holy Christ. There is no way, shape or form what you saw for just those few seconds wasn't your Chicky's. This was somebody's major screw-up and you don't like the awful feeling that it was maybe yours.

You point at Dan and the words aren't coming out. He knows what you are trying to say though.

"Fuck you Scott, it's not my fault," he blurts out.

"Are you kidding me?" You are irate. "Didn't you tell them where to find the goddamn bomb?" You are shouting. Hale puts his hand on your shoulder and a finger up to his lips. He is right. Someone could hear you. Now is not the time for panic.

You drop your voice down to a whisper. "Didn't you?"

"Scott, I read back everything you wrote verbatim just like a fuckin' parrot. I told them the fuckin' thing was in the men's room."

"Oh shit," you say, mostly to yourself.

"It was in the men's room, right Scott?"

You just stare at him.

"Oh Christ Scott, tell me it was in the men's room."

All you can do is stare blankly at him. You want to tell him yes. Dammit, you want for that thing to have been in the goddamned men's room, and it would have been if it wasn't for Grandpa Dump reading the whole sports section in there.

"Nikko." Dan's voice gets higher. "Tell me you guys put it in the men's room."

"No," you finally tell him. "It wasn't."

"What?"

"It was in some kind of mop closet next to the bathrooms," Nikko says. "We couldn't get into the men's room."

Dan's jaw drops open. "This isn't my fault, guys. This is not my fuckin' fault!"

"It's not my fault either," you say, looking at Nikko. In a way you know it could be but only to the extent that putting the bomb in the mop closet was your idea. If there is a most blameable person here, it is painfully obvious that you have become the most likely candidate.

"Scott, nobody said it was your fault," Hale tells you. You are looking at Nikko to say something but he doesn't. He is probably as much to blame as you but he isn't about to pony up to that one.

"Look, I don't even know what really happened. That thing wasn't supposed to even be close to detonating until after nine," Nikko says.

"Fried fuckin' chicken," Dan says. You just stare at the floor.

Hale slaps the side of the TV. The reception is fuzzing out. "I hate this fucking thing," he says.

Dan lights up like someone has flicked the on switch in his head. "Wait," he says. "The news station. The one I called. Put that on."

You sit and listen. It doesn't take long to hear their version of what happened and they are all over the story. And why shouldn't they be? It's their scoop and you had given it to them. You listen to the voices coming from the speakers.

"...we're going to be sticking with the live coverage of an apparent terrorist bombing in the downtown shopping district of Beverly Hills. No word yet on the full extent of the damage but let's go live with Terry Baldini at the scene in the KNGW Newscopter. Can you hear me, Terry?"

"Peter, we're right above the blaze on Beverly Drive and fire crews are trying to fight this massive blaze allegedly caused by the terrorist bomb. From what I can see up here, the entire front of the building is mostly in ruins and there appears to have been some casualties. I can see several ambulances on the street and it looks like there may have been a tour bus of some sort parked in front of the Chicky's restaurant or the bagel store which are both completely engulfed in flames at the moment. The tour bus has been moved over to the other side of Beverly Drive so that fire crews can bring their equipment up to the front of the building. I'm not sure at this moment if anyone from the tour bus was even in the building at the time of the explosion or if there was even anyone aboard the tour bus at the time either, but there does appear to be a number of casualties that the EMT's are tending to as I speak."

Christ, the damn thing had gone off somehow before anyone could find it and the whole building had gone up. Maybe it wasn't your fault. Maybe some dumbass cop pulled opened up the door with a cigarette hanging out of his mouth. You want to think that but there is no way. Even if someone else had set the stupid thing off, fault lay squarely with you for putting it there to begin with.

You never thought that it could go this far but for some reason it doesn't seem like the other guys are as frightened as you are. You can tell the feeling in the room—that you had created an even bigger news event—was electric for them. It was compelling, just like when the space shuttle fell out of the sky in pieces. In a way, you feel yourself getting caught in the downward spiral of insanity that makes you get a little bit excited along with them. You can feel the rush creeping in and although it is disgusting to you, you don't do a damn thing to stop it.

Hale seems to have lost interest in the radio drama and is looking for his dope. He finds it and packs another bowl and takes a big hit from the bong before passing it to you.

"You know, as far as anyone knows, they're saying that it was a terrorist bomb," Nikko tells the room. "The whole thing worked, don't you see?"

"What are you saying? That they bought it?" you ask.

"Sure. At least that's what the radio said. It's out of our hands. It's done." He reaches over and high-fives with Dan.

Having it out of your hands isn't really reassuring. Especially since the reporter says that there may have been casualties. You wonder what the hell a tour bus was doing there at that time of night anyway.

"Aren't you concerned that more people may have been killed?" you ask him.

"Look man," he says calmly. "Maybe somebody got killed in there. Shit, maybe a bunch of people got killed. We didn't do it on purpose. The important thing here is no one will ever trace Bo back to us. Especially not now. Even if we did put the bomb in the wrong room and Dan called a half an hour late, it's not like we did it on purpose, right? The point is that we did it and it's done and regardless of the fact that it doesn't exactly end up the way we had planned, it does the trick. We're out from under Bo. Don't you see?"

He is justifying the whole thing and you are buying it. Hell, you want to buy it. You are a willing consumer of the propaganda.

"Bottom line here," Nikko adds, swallowing hard. "By killing Bo you jeopardized all of our futures and now you're out of it." He looks over at you and so does Hale. There is something about it you just don't like too much.

You realize he did just put Bo's death squarely on you. The truth comes out. This is a first. He can see in your eyes that you understand what he is saying.

"Scott, look, Bo was a fucking accident. So was killing anybody in that slum building and so was tonight. I'm not tossing my life away because some lowlife, jarhead prick dies on your floor."

"Me neither," Dan jumps in.

"Hey," Hale says, putting his hand on your shoulder. It seems like everyone was touching you a lot lately. In a way it kind of makes you feel uncomfortable. "It's done, it's over. I'm not worried about the bomb. I'm more concerned that we don't exactly have an alibi this time," he says to you.

"You're right, not for tonight at least," you tell him, trying to listen to him, the radio and take a hit at the same time.

"Sure we do," Nikko says. "The pizza delivery guy saw us."

"No," Hale says. "The pizza guy saw me and you. Scott was in the can and Dan ran back to his room to get money."

"Fuck, we are stupid, we should have made sure he saw all of us," says Dan. He has a point. The pizza guy came around nine and if your damn bladder wasn't the size of a goddamned peanut then you would have been here too. Shit, now that you think of it, if you hadn't taken the time to check out your haircut in the mirror like some vain chump, you might have even passed him in the hall as he was leaving.

"I know it's kind of too late but we could pop over to Willington. I know we should probably watch the news but this way we'll make sure people see us at the movie," you say.

"It's not great but I guess it's something," Nikko says. "It'll have to do."

"Wait." Hale pops a tape into the VCR and quickly starts programming it with the remote. "I'll tape the ten o'clock news and the eleven o' clock too. We'll watch it later."

"Hand me the bong," Dan says to you. "I got a fuckin' idea."

He takes it from you, lights a big hit and proceeds to blow the smoke all over his shirt. You don't know what to think about the whole thing. You are all half-crazy at that point and dropping fast.

"What the hell are you doing? You're going to reek of pot," Nikko says to him, equally as perplexed as you are.

"That's the whole point," Dan explains, handing the bong to Hale. "Whoever sees us will just think we spent the whole evening in here baking. Anybody who knows any of us wouldn't even think twice about it. Scott's become quite the little pothead lately so nobody would expect anything less from him either."

This is slowly becoming kick Scott in the ass night. However, it isn't totally untrue though. You smoked a lot more dope this past week than all of last semester, hell, even more than some small countries, and maybe some of what happened really was your fault. You always pick on Dan anyway so maybe it's your turn for lumps.

Hale shrugs and follows Fuckin' Dan's lead, inhaling a lungful of dope just to blow it out onto himself. Nikko does the same and finally you. Just to be on the safe side you go around again before heading over to Willington.

The movie is packed. *Heavy Metal* is one of those rare flicks that, although it isn't really that good of a movie, certainly makes up for it in sheer fucking cool. You'll never forget the time you saw it in high school with a bunch of bike gang buddies and a case of beer someone's brother had gotten for you. At first, you thought it was going to be some dumbass cartoon like Bakshi's *Hobbit* or that horrible piece of shit *American Pop,* but the moment the movie started with Sammy Hagar blasting and that Trans-Am dropping out of the spaceship you knew this flick was going to be pretty badass. A double feature like this was bound to bring out everybody, especially those who would be afraid that they'd be considered geeks for not going. On this campus they were legion.

Fuck, all the better. Like with the Stonehouse fire alarm you wanted to be seen by as many people as possible. You get there late and the lights are down and the picture has just started. You missed the whole Trans-Am thing which bites your bag. Yeah, it's kind of stupid but it's your favorite part of the whole movie.

You look around for Mooch or Snatch or anybody you know but it's too dark to see so you just take four seats in the back. You can't hear too well, which is why the only people sitting around you are the underclassmen neckers. It doesn't really matter that much, you don't feel like being here, but it's all part of the big show. It occurs to you how you've been spending practically every waking moment of the past few days with these guys, with the exception of your trip to Mulholland, your haircut and your entirely half-hearted attempts at working out. You like these guys a lot but maybe it was time to find something else to occupy your time. Something to keep you away from smoking so much dope. Baseball was an option. You could try to get back on the team, but that would mean getting your personal shit together snap, snap. From the smoke your throat feels like someone worked it over with fifty grit sandpaper. You get up to go for a Coke.

"Anybody want anything?" you ask, maybe a little bit too loudly but the neckers don't even notice.

"M & M's, the peanut ones," Dan says. "Or Reese's Pieces. Something I can throw at those little fuckers sucking face over there."

Peanut M & M's? God, you can't believe he actually likes that shit.

You hold your hand out while he reluctantly hands over a buck. "How about you guys?"

"Christ," Nikko says, looking over at the couple making out ten feet away. "I haven't seen pussy in so long, I'd probably throw stones at it."

Hale just sticks his tongue out and flashes your little hand sign. You flash it back and head for the candy table. Dan's Elvis-meets-Motley Crue hand thing has become de-rigueur lately and you think it's kind of cool. Like one of those Rat Pack things. Kind of like if the King did a movie about going to hell. *Hellvis.* That's how *he'd* point to everybody throughout the whole movie. In a month it would be as out as *The Osbornes*, but for now you feel like you need the little gang hand sign.

The fire still hangs in the back of your mind like the sour memory of a bad date. You aren't going to think about it. For the next two hours you are going to try to focus on the movie. You are going to think about baseball. You are going to think about getting your ass back into your schoolwork. You are going to think about Manny and you are going to think about... Jackie.

She isn't exactly the last person you expect to see here but she'd make the top three—if you considered Bo as well, maybe it's top four. But, there she is, standing with her back turned and she can't see you. Oh God. You knew you'd have to bump into her sometime and you weren't sure this was the right moment. You feel the need to say something to her. If she walks away without you even trying you know you'll feel like shit and obsess about it the whole night. You know the best thing would be to forget you even saw her and avoid her entirely. The little voice in your head tells you to just turn the hell around and go back to your goddamned seat.

You go to her anyway.

Hearing the footsteps come up behind her, she turns around as you get near.

"Scott?"

The indifference in how she speaks your name—lacking all of the familiarity and warmth of having been together for two years —reminds you of the way she'd probably greet a stalker or talk about a zit on her ass. You can tell she is nervous, especially since you kind of snuck up behind her. You never want to bump into

your ex without some sort of warning and here you are like a puff
of smoke.

You take a deep breath. Even though you had a moment to
think about it, you still have no idea what to say to her. She looks
good but a fawning compliment from you would be completely
wrong at this moment. You really want to say something though.
Man, she really does look great.

"Uh, hi, I was on my way to get a Coke and I saw you here."

She doesn't seem to really care, she looks at you like you are
the opposite of civilization.

"What the hell did you do to your hair? It looks shitty."

She wrinkles her nose, and then does something that strikes
you as being quite openly hostile. She puts two fingers on your
chest and pushes you away from her a little bit.

"Christ, and you reek of pot," she adds. "I've heard that you've
become quite the chronic lately."

This certainly isn't going as well as you hoped. You might as
well have painted the name *Titanic* in giant letters on your ass. All
hands abandon ship, you've hit an iceberg named Jackie and
you're sinking like a ten-pound stone.

It is one of those times when you wish you just had the sense
to say *Fuck You* and walk away like Hale's brother Dave did at his
wedding. She is picking you apart like a vulture on a carcass and
you are taking it. It's all part of your self-destructive nature. It's
almost like you want to see yourself fail sometimes because failure
is so much easier to achieve than success.

"Jackie, I was hoping that you and I could, uh, get together
and talk." It comes out of your mouth like a street vagrant asking
for a dime.

She shakes her head even before you can finish the sentence.
You spent two years together and said that you loved one another
countless times. She was a big part of your life and you thought
you'd been a big part of hers too and now here she is treating you
like some kind of virus.

"Look Scott," she says coldly. "It's too late. It's more than
obvious you'll never change."

Jesus H. How the fuck do you respond to that? Of course it's a trick question. If you say *yes, I can change, I was an asshole before and now I won't be,* then you're just full of shit in her eyes. You are pathetic and desperate. If you answer *no,* then all the bad shit she ever believed about you is true. Damned if you do, damned if you don't. You might as well stick a goddamned fork in your ass because brother, you are big time done.

Like a complete jackass, you try to say something in your defense but before you can, someone comes out of the bathroom to your left and walks towards you. You sort of recognize him as Todd something or other from Tau Delta and when he gets close enough, Jackie grabs his hand.

"Scott, we have to go," she says. And with that you watch them walk out together.

They were obviously here on a date together and now they're hoofing so he can take her back to his room and make time with her while you just stand there like a chump. You've gone down in flames before but this makes the Hindenburg look like a weenie-roast. Seeing them together feels like getting whacked in the face with a two-by-four. The stupid part of you wants to follow them but you've made enough of a fool of yourself for one night. There is no doubt about it whatsoever. It's over. All that time together and you are a maggot on a birthday cake to her. Your heart sinks.

You stand in the hall not knowing what to do with yourself for a very long time. The inside of your chest feels raw as if someone has cut you open using the rusty lid off of a cat food can. Your head feels enormously heavy, like the earth is just sucking it towards the ground. You think it's fairly obvious, there is no one to blame for this but yourself. You should have listened to that little voice in your head when it said to walk away. There you are, looking for the reasons why things had gotten so screwed up and all you needed to do to find the smoking gun was to gaze down at your own trembling hand.

The girls at the concession stand saw everything. It was certainly the most exciting thing happening in this hallway so who could blame them? Certainly not you. You just smile and get yourself a jumbo Coke and a big bag of Peanut M's while they uncomfortably smile back. You can almost sense they want to say something. You think they might too, so you pay quickly and leave without a word. You go back into the movie and hand Dan his candy and just sit there watching the screen without saying anything. The only thought in your head is that next time you'll know better than to stick your face into a meat grinder. At least you hope you'll know better next time. Why is there always a sneaking suspicion that you won't?

ONE4

The carnage is magnificent. The anchor people and reporters spend a lot of time talking about what had happened because this was news with a capital *N*, the kind that they all dream about in a world where the sorrow and sadness of everyday life are the brick and mortar that careers are built with. In a world where the worst things that people do to other people became a spectator sport, this was huge. Downtown Beverly Hills had suffered a terrorist attack apparently by a group calling themselves *The Doomsday Club* and the results were breathtaking. Twenty-two people, mostly retired tourists from Germany had lost their lives in a blast that police had been warned about only twenty minutes beforehand. The two officers on the scene were killed instantly as were five employees of Chicky's Chicken Kitchen restaurant and the driver of the charter bus.

Police suspected a bomb placed in proximity to a gas main caused an explosion that destroyed the entire building and shattered windows up and down the block.

Radio station KGNW-AM had reported that an unidentified male caller phoned in the bomb threat to their station, minutes before it went off. The station notified the police immediately and by the time officers arrived to investigate, it was too late.

The unidentified caller did not claim responsibility for the bombing but named a person or persons working under the name The Doomsday Club as the allegedly responsible party. According to this caller, The Doomsday Club was also responsible for the earlier firebombing of an abandoned apartment building that took the lives of at least five victims. The terrorists further claim that these attacks are the result of God's judgement upon a world full of "greed and sloth." The police force has issued a twenty-four hour tactical alert in Downtown Los Angeles. The FBI has been brought in and a spokesperson for the President of the United States has publicly denounced this attack as cowardly and reprehensible and wishes to assure everyone in the greater L.A. area, and the country, that whomever is responsible will be brought to justice.

You watch the TV in shock. Hearing about it on the radio doesn't have nearly the same impact as does seeing the flames leap dozens of feet into the sky and the score of firemen trying in vain to control the blaze. Your magic beans certainly lit up the entire building and as you come to learn from the newscast, there indeed was a natural gas line that fed Chicky's and the Bagelry from a junction in the mop closet. Alone, the acetylene bomb would have blown out that hallway and set the roof ablaze. With the help of the gas line, the entire building became an instant cloud of fire, blowing out all of the walls and windows with the force of a hurricane. Twenty of the tour group escaped death only to suffer burns, cuts and broken bones when the force of the blast hit them as they hurried on board the bus. Some of the Germans intended for this to be the trip of a lifetime. You certainly made sure of that.

You fill your lungs continually with smoke from the bong as you watch over and over the massive amount of damage you have created. It is, in one word, *prettyfuckinghorrible*. There are more people dead but that refuses to register in your mind. You are still completely fixated on the painful encounter with Jackie.

Dan's face has turned ashen and Hale refuses to even look at the screen anymore but Nikko, he is glued to it. You still are unable to believe the story on the TV has anything at all to do with you. All of your actions were done with no intention of hurting anyone but something had gone seriously wrong. Jackie's actions were done knowing that she was hurting you and it doesn't seem to bother her one bit. The faultline of your sanity is full of shifting sand.

You can wake up one morning, walk out to the store to get a quart of milk and get hit by a bullet fired by a man trying to scare away an attacker a half a mile down the street. It strikes you in the neck and you fall to the sidewalk and die not ever knowing what happened. The person who fired that gun never intended to hurt anyone but acted in self-defense. But you, you're still stone dead because you just happened to be in the wrong place at the wrong time, and your reward for that is a nap in the dirt.

"We have to turn ourselves in," you say.

Nikko snaps his head toward you first. As does Hale and Dan.

"No way. No, no, fucking no!" Nikko says. "We cop to this and we're gonna get the needle."

Silent, Hale nods his head. Dan squeezes the bridge of his nose.

"We just play it cool and we can get out of this," Hale says quietly. "We shouldn't all have to pay for this. It was a mistake."

You don't like the way he said *all*.

"We're so totally safe," Nikko says. "We pulled this shit off flawlessly. Nobody will ever suspect us, Scott. Don't you see how fucking cool this is?"

No, you don't. Bit by bit, as you tumble down into the pit of self-discovery, you can't bear to look at what you were seeing. You retreat into the one place that seems both the most comforting and least horrible, the inside of a bong. As you smoke more and more, your thoughts are consumed with death and life and why the two defining events of a person's existence can happen without so much as a solid reason or warning. There is nothing concrete about it at all, especially the disturbing thought that not a single thing in life is permanent, not even life itself. Your thoughts drift from profane to profound and all points in between. You continue to inhale more and more smoke because you believe with all your heart that it might somehow free you from the torment of eventually facing up to the consequences of your actions. You are suffering a spiritual death and as hard as you attempt to make it feel like an examination of your soul, the only thing you will come out of this with is a head full of fucking horrible nightmares.

You grab Nikko by the front of his shirt. "What the fuck have we done? What the fuck have we done?"

Dan pulls you off him.

"You're fucking losing it, Scott! Losing it!" Nikko hisses while Hale calms him down. Dan sits you down on your bed and Hale produces an Ambien from the bottle he stole off his stepmom. You lay back on your pillow as he softly tells you, "It's gonna be okay. It's gonna be okay."

In your dreams, it is finally made clear where you've been falling from all of those previous times. You had come to believe that it was from a cliff or the top of a building or an airplane. It couldn't have been more obvious though that it was never any of these. Your fall is from grace.

You awaken in the middle of the night lying on your bed fully dressed and your head feels like a demolition derby. Nikko and Fuckin' Dan are gone and Hale is snoring lightly over on his side of the room. You get up in the dark, pull off your clothes and cry yourself back to sleep. It doesn't matter if Hale hears you or not. You think it's fairly obvious that you and he aren't made of the same mettle. You don't feel like you have to prove anything by not crying. He just keeps snoring though and eventually you begin falling again.

In what is no more than the dawn of semi-consciousness, Hale has his hand on your shoulder and is speaking. As best he can, there is an explanation about your future, all of your futures and the answer is painfully obvious. Most of all, he describes the part you are going to have to play, the assumption of responsibility and the inevitable atonement and penance for what you have done. Although you don't understand at first, he explains the situation and you try to accept the fact that when the time came, all would be clear to you. Your sleep after that is fitful and labored, maybe your sub-conscious mind understood how very unprepared you would be for the events that were to follow.

The knock on the door comes at a seemingly obscene time of the morning. Light pours in through the window but it feels harsh and unfriendly. Somehow you manage to spill out of bed onto your feet without falling. To say you feel pretty ragged is an understatement; it is more like someone has tied you to the back of a car and spent a long evening joyriding a dirt road with you hooked to the bumper. You look over at Hale's bed and he is gone already. With your luck the jerk at the door is probably Mooch or Snatch or some dipshit friend of Hale's. You start to think whoever is waking you better hope you're feeling too shitty to rip them a new one.

The two men in cheap suits standing at the door watch you curiously with what must be perpetual stonefaced stares. When you see the badge that one of them holds up, the shock of seeing a pair of police detectives standing in front of you is like having a bolt of lightning shoot up your ass.

Guess what dickhead? You're fucked, the little voice in your head tells you. This is it. Hale wasn't here because those shitheels had turned you in. You are speechless. Those guys saw a liferaft and bailed like rats from a sinking ship. Fuck women and children first, this had obviously turned into every man for himself, a perfect example of Social Darwinism. Your very own friends had obviously scapegoated you and you were about to get your sorry ass dragged downtown by two bad suits. You'd be locked away until the day they strapped you to that table and killed you.

For a second you think you can turn tail and make a run for it, diving through the window by Hale's bed. If it was spring and warm out, it would have been opened all the way but like yesterday it was only cracked and you'd have to crash through the glass first, probably lacerating your head, neck, body and legs so badly that the best landing you'd be able to manage is one that brought your face into the sidewalk with the most brutal example of gravity in action. Either that, or since you can't remember in that split-second whether the window is plexiglass or not, you'd just take the risk of bouncing off of it like a superball. It isn't until the cop nearest to you starts talking that you are able to push your idiotic urge to flee aside long enough to get hold of your senses.

"Morning. We're Detectives Martinez and Sheppard. We're investigating the disappearance of Richard Boyd, the West Wing Resident Assistant."

The fogginess in your brain lifts immediately but the grogginess in your body remains. The net result of hearing those words makes your head snap back as if the cop had socked you in the jaw with a bag full of nickels. You notice a hint of curiosity in his granite stare; your loopy behavior has piqued his interest. Your tank is empty and running on fumes but you have the presence of mind to just make him think you are another dipshit college student, which really isn't a stretch by any means.

In the dark recesses of your mind you imagine yourself putting your hands out in front of you and saying to them.

I did it, I killed the dumb sonofabitch. I killed everybody.

It would be a relief. In a way you know it would. The cops would look at each other stunned for a moment, and you'd repeat your impassioned confession for them again.

Hey you, asshole with the badge. Stupid, deaf, flatfoot, dumbass, I said I beat the life out of the jarhead cocksmoke. What in Christ are you waiting for? Me, to off you two lazy pig fucks as well?

Instead you open your mouth and repeat what Manny had told you.

"The rumor going around is that he was abducted by a, you know, spacecraft or something."

Momentarily, you watch the cop clench his jaw. It is obvious that you aren't the first person today to have enlightened them with this stunning revelation. To your relief, he chooses not to pursue it much further.

"Do you have a roommate?"

"Yeah, but he must have left before I got up. He might be in the library or something." Yeah, right, Hale might go to the library if he found out they were giving out nickel bags with every copy of *Catcher in the Rye* but what were you going to tell the cops? That he was out scoring some narf, try back in a half-hour? Instead you say, "Why? Do you think he may have been abducted by a UFO also?"

You can tell right away that a box lunch has more of a sense of humor than these two. You always run into people like that. You swear it has to be bad luck.

"If you happen to hear anything or remember anything that may be relevant, here's my card. My precinct phone number and cell number are on it. Thanks for your time, go back to bed."

"Yeah," you say, as earnestly as possible as you take the card from him. "I'll do that."

Shutting the door, you let the cops vanish from your sight and your head drops to your chest. They are miles away from anything that should cause you worry but it seems like a veritable singeing of your shorthairs. If you hadn't been feeling like shit you might have tried to think too much and probably would have said something even more stupid. As it was, you are sure you will only appear as just another dumbass kid in any notes they might have been taking.

You look down at the card in your hand. Dick Martinez, Detective, LAPD. How about that? You guess all the Dicks stick together.

The thought occurs to just rip up the card, just having it around makes you feel really uncomfortable. Instead you toss it onto your desk.

Another thought crosses your mind, a thought about your future, of what might happen in your future if you don't start taking the reigns again. During the past few days you've lost your sense of having any control over your destiny anymore. The decisions you've been making lately were almost completely influenced by the guys, and the guys were just flying by the seat of their collective Levis. You were trying to dig your way out of a hole and all that was going to get you was deeper in shit and eventually, buried alive. There was no way on God's green earth that you were going to take the fall alone for any of this. You all had to take the heat. That was the only way.

In a bizarre way it occurs to you that if you had surrendered to the police and told them that you killed Bo by accident, you'd be in a hell of a lot less trouble than if you got pinched for the firebombings. As long as they never connected the two, you could just say you panicked and dumped Bo in the Pacific Ocean. You could probably just take a minimum sentence or walk with a slap on the wrist for involuntary manslaughter or killing an asshole without a license.

You might just have broken down and done it. The problem was there were other variables in this equation named Dan, Hale and Nikko. A jury wouldn't have too tough of a time reserving you a seat in old sparky. Someone would tip the DA off and he'd bring Jackie in as a character witness to testify. If that happened then Stephen Hawking had a better chance of walking than you did. You'd be toast for sure.

Your watch says it's after ten, which is much later than you originally thought it was when the Hardy Boys showed up. As far as you could remember from last night, nobody was looking for you, at least not yet. You have a real vague idea where Hale is but that's alright. You are going to run a couple of errands. A nugget of a half-assed backup plan starts to form in your head. You are going to need something downtown to pull it off. It was better that nobody else knew where you were headed anyway. You toss on some clothes and your hat and grab your keys.

First, you hit an ATM and drain what is left in your account, pick up a paper and then you are going to find this guy Snatch is always talking about. Even though nobody is around, you still feel like you have to sneak out of the building.

You are so preoccupied with what you need to do and where you need to go, that you don't notice misssing is Nikko's five-year old black Mazda 323 that was parked next to you yesterday. Even if you did, the significance of knowing that the wheels of your escape are in motion wouldn't have changed a thing anyway.

ONE5

The directions you got from Snatch are lousy at best but you find the place you're looking for all the same. The guy you have to talk to full-on denies knowing your drug dealing dirtbag buddy but who can blame him? Instead, you re-acquaint him with someone he's definitely heard of before: Ulysses S. Grant. You don't care. What he has for you is definitely worth fifty bucks.

On your way out, you drop a quarter in a rusty old newspaper box and pick up today's issue of the Times. No surprise, there it is, black and white and read all over. TERRORIST BOMB KILLS 25 IN BEVERLY HILLS is printed so big on the front page you could have read it from orbit. Looking at it, at the picture of the building being consumed by the blaze, your chest tightens up and you can't feel any shittier than you do right now.

"This isn't happening," you mutter to yourself. It comes out more like a desperate chant that you hope will turn back time like Christopher Reeve does at the end of *Superman*. If only life were that easy. Even the Man of Steel had to fly around the earth and turn it backwards to do that and here you are, just hoping that three little words are going to fix everything up. Your reality is virtual, at best.

The paper doesn't tell you anything you don't already know. The facts are simple; there was a bomb, it killed twenty-five people, responsibility was claimed by a terrorist group calling themselves The Doomsday Club and the suspects are still at large. You fold it up and are going to toss it into the garbage. You want to, as if doing so could make the whole thing just disappear. Instead, you think twice about it and throw the paper into the passenger seat of the Civic. The guys had probably seen it already but you want to bring it back for them anyway. The way they had been acting lately, especially Nikko, you wouldn't be surprised if one of those crazy bastards had already started a scrapbook.

There is something gnawing away at your insides and you try like hell to convince yourself it's because you haven't eaten anything yet. You stop at Del Taco and order a bagful of some fake mex. L.A. is the kind of town where you can't toss a rock without hitting a little bodega that serves authentic style tacos and not this drive-thru window shit. In this neighborhood, most of those little grease joints look pretty scary so you stick with the cookie-cutter gringo stuff.

Four tacos and a large diet Pepsi kill most of the drive home. You slurp down the last of your drink as you pull back onto Campus Drive and promise to only patronize fast-food joints that serve Coke instead. The fake mex is going to sit in your gut like a cannonball and you hope that Hale has some more Tums back in the room. He always did; antacids truly were life preservers for children of the rich.

When you get back to campus you take a long look at the thing you picked up downtown before jamming it into your back pocket and grabbing the newspaper from the seat next to you. If Nikko was around he'd think you popped out to just pick it up and you wouldn't get any third degree from him. It's not like he was the kind of guy that would do that to you but for some reason you had developed that kind of suspicion about each other last night. It was obvious, especially after the guys let you know in their own special passive-aggressive way that somehow this whole abortion was your fault in the first place. There was no doubt in your mind that if some kind of dumbass game of musical chairs went down you were going to be the one standing there with his dick in his hand when the music stopped playing.

Last night you kept your mouth shut, figuring it would only lead to bad otherwise. Come on, if you really wanted to pin blame, you could probably trace it back to Dan winking at the Beckster in the quad that third week of school last year. That was the seed of your troubles right there but were you going to point fingers? No.

As you turn down your hall, your cell phone starts to ring. The number is blocked. You know who it is. You fumble with the keys in your pocket. Finally, you get the door open with your less than nimble fingers and grab the call on the third ring.

Before you can even say hello you are greeted by the sharp sound of Hale's voice.

"'The fuck are you? Why are you out of breath?"

You have to wonder if his Christmas cards are that warm and fuzzy.

"Getting a paper and a taco. Have you seen the front page of the Times?" The connection is bad like he was dialing from Mars. "Hey, it sounds like you're calling from your ass."

"Dude, we're just a couple of miles away. We have a problem. We thought you took off too."

Too? Problem? What he means is initially lost on you. You guess your silence is question enough for Hale.

"Nikko's gone," he says. You still didn't get the importance of this.

"Gone?"

"Yeah, he took off this morning sometime real early."

"Wait, what do you mean?" You are still perplexed. What the hell was he getting at?

"Vegas," Hale says. "The fucker went to Las Vegas."

"Wait, how do you know?"

You can hear Hale say something to somebody else and you pick up Dan's voice in the background. It's muffled and it seems like Hale has his hand over the mouthpiece which strikes you as odd. You let it pass and you can hear the rustling of paper.

"He left a note," Hale says. "It says: Dan, gone to Vegas to settle that score. Sevens, J."

"Sevens?" None of this is making any sense to you at all. "What's *Sevens*?"

"I dunno," Hale says. "He used it as a salutary like you'd use *sincerely* or *best wishes* or *go blow yourself*. He wrote sevens because he's going to Vegas. Scott, that's not the point."

You have Hale read the note again. To anyone else it would have been like trying to figure out Chinese arithmetic but you understand it perfectly knowing Nikko the way you do.

Last spring, Nikko and a couple of guys who were seniors at the time took a road trip to play a little blackjack after a heated debate on ways to beat a six-deck shoe using math. They get there and head to the Grand Tropic Hotel right off the strip because one of the other guys knows somebody whose uncle could get them a comped room for one night. After check in, they hit the ATM and each guy pulls out his wad of five-hundred bucks apiece. The bet between them was whoever came out with the most cash in four hours got a hundred bucks from the other two guys. A hundred bucks says that you're the best blackjack player and you're only going to risk five-hundred to prove it. Alright, maybe you're not as smart as Nikko by a longshot but when he told you about it, you could see stupid written all over it with spray paint.

So Nikko had this completely half-assed card counting scam that he was going to try to pull in a town that took cheats out into the desert and left them in a shallow hole. Sometimes smart guys weren't so goddamned smart, you know? He spent the first hour looking for the right table, one without too many people and a card shoe that was practically empty. At first he didn't see one but way in the back he saw a dealer shuffling cards and getting ready to start a whole new shoe. He walked over, put a hundred bucks on the table and got himself dealt in. The dealer gave Nikko the cut so he placed the marker way at the back of the deck, maybe twenty cards from the end.

Now, although he explained the whole thing a thousand times, you never really cared too much to pay full attention. From all of the tellings though you knew the basics of counting cards relied on keeping track of how many face cards and tens have been dealt and using natural laws of probability to figure when one may get dealt next—those were called point cards. You do this with one deck of cards or two and you may even stand a chance, but the casinos aren't stupid. That's why they play with six whole decks all jumbled together at the same time. The way Nikko described it, you were still going to end up with an average of about four point cards for every thirteen dealt, but keeping track of ninety-six face cards and tens was a nightmare at best. Nobody tries it, nobody in their right mind that is.

But Nikko thought he was smart enough to beat any system they could devise to keep him from coming out ahead. He thought deep down inside he was going to beat the house by outsmarting them. While a six-deck shoe was as incomprehendable to the average human mind as is particle physics it was supposed to be child's play to someone like Nikko. Someone who was a particle physicist.

Now, the thing about counting cards or gathering any sort of statistical data is that you can't use it until enough information has been doled out to you. This meant Nikko was going to have to play like everyone else until at least three decks had been dealt out. The odds were as much against him as they were every other schmo in the joint. He knew the first couple hundred dollars of his stake would be the sacrificial lambs of his flock. Getting through three decks would take nine or ten hands with four other players at the table and since this was twenty five dollar minimum, two hundred fifty would be just fine.

As he figured, he lost more cash than he won in the first ten hands of the game. On pure luck he managed a string of four wins in a row but got greedy and blew it on the next hand. Even so, he was only a hundred and eighty bucks behind, way ahead of where he thought he'd be. Honestly, he didn't even notice though because he was too busy trying to keep track of all of the point cards that had come up so far and, to his recollection, the back half of the shoe was going to be loaded with them.

So then he began betting more aggressively. At first, losing another hundred within the space of three hands and then his luck started to turn. On the next hand he bet fifty bucks on the feeling that a dose of point cards should be coming his way and boom, Queen-Ace. Blackjack. As the dealer hit the last couple of decks in the shoe Nikko was ripping it up. The cards were coming his way. He was still behind but with some really heavy betting on the last few hands he began thinking he was going to walk away with enough dough to really show those other guys what's what.

Now don't think this all wasn't being noticed. Casinos love you when you drop your paycheck in their joint but if you start to win, even a little, you're going to arouse their suspicions because the odds are so much against you to begin with. Gambling is just that—gambling. Even the lottery is gambling and all that is, when you think about it, is a tax on those who are really, incredibly bad at math.

Spotting a counter in a casino is a lot like finding the Snoopy balloon in the Macy's parade, and those who do it for a living can do it in their sleep. Nikko was way too easy to find. After watching him for one more hand to be sure, the pit boss stepped in and closed the table.

Nikko was pissed. How dare they? Just when things were ready to break open for him. He thought of lodging a complaint but totally chickened out and decided to go find another table instead. Before he could leave, the pit boss quietly leaned over to him and told him that it was in his best interest to just take his chips and leave the casino and if they ever caught Nikko card counting in here again, he'd be one sorry motherfucker. Without saying a thing, Nikko grabbed his money and bolted like his ass was on fire.

He took his chips to the cashier and to his shock found that he only had four hundred and fifty bucks, fifty less than he walked in with. All that work and he still lost. Man, was he pissed. He took his money and went to the lobby to lick his wounds and bumped into one of the guys he came with. Turns out, that guy lost all of his wad in the first ten minutes trying some really dumb scam that he read about on the internet. Together they go up to the room and there's the third guy just sitting on the bed, eating room service and watching HBO. It turns out that this guy didn't even go to the casino at all, he just figured that Nikko and the other guy would both lose all of their money and he'd still have his original five-hundred that he showed up with and thus, win the bet.

Nikko went absolutely ballistic about this. But the guy reminded him that the bet was *whoever had the most money left after four hours wins* and after spending twenty bucks on room service the other guy still had four-hundred and eighty bucks on him, thirty more than Nikko. The bet they made never really said that anyone had to gamble. Nikko couldn't believe he was going to lose after he proved to himself that his card counting scam could work. He looked at his watch and realized he had over fifty minutes left before the four hours were up so he ran out of the room and went across the street to another casino where he lost another three hundred in half an hour before calling it quits. He went back to the room a beaten man. Beaten but really, really pissed.

The joker who won the bet let Nikko and the other dude off the hook telling them he had only done it to try and make a point —that gambling was a loser's path. Nikko spent the rest of the night lying on the bed, staring at the ceiling, absolutely seething with anger.

When Nikko got back to school, all anyone heard about for weeks and weeks was him go on about having been cheated out of the money he should have won. It got to the point where you almost didn't even want to hang out with him anymore because you were sick of hearing him rant like a childish madman who couldn't stand having the chip knocked off of his shoulder even once. You were all pretty damn sick as shit of hearing about it and you were finally going to say something to him. Before you could though, boom, like magic, one day he stopped talking about it altogether and that was the last any of you had heard about it. Not since today.

You keep thinking about the note over and over. If this week were some kind of goddamned movie it could have been titled *Nothing Good is Going to Come of This*. You have an icy-bad feeling that there isn't going to be a happy ending any time soon. Sevens. You hope there'll be enough sevens to go around this time.

After Hale reads the note a second time, you jot it down word-for-word on a piece of paper and nervously keep turning it over in your hands. You stare at it like it has become the center of the universe, which for you, it has.

"Hold on a second," Hale tells you and the phone changes hands.

"I found it under my door this morning," Dan says, his voice getting a little shaky. "I'm just glad my fuckin' roommate didn't see it first."

"What time did you find it?"

"Eight-ish. I got up to take a leak and saw it on the floor. I was so out of it that I didn't think twice about it. I just read it and put it on my dresser. It didn't even hit me what it meant until I popped awake again around nine."

You check your watch. It was almost one in the afternoon. If Nikko left before eight, even if he stopped to piss and gas up, he was probably already there.

"Nikko's roommate told us he was there around two which is right about the time he left your room after you crashed," Dan was explaining to you. "He said that Nikko fell asleep for a half-hour and then grabbed his knapsack and took off for his lab. The roommate didn't think it was strange because Nikko is always taking off and going over there in the middle of the night."

Well that answers that question, you think to yourself. If he went to his lab then you could be pretty sure that he was headed back to Vegas with more than just a wad of cash this time. "Tell him the other bad news," you hear Hale say.

Oh Christ, there's more? Your mind races through what other bad things could have happened, the list is too long to pick only one.

"Don't tell me," you say. "Bo's back from the dead."

Suddenly Dan goes silent like a rock. Whatever it was, you must have hit a nerve.

"Not exactly,"

"Not exactly? What the hell does that mean?"

"Nikko lifted Bo's wallet and credit cards sometime before we burned him up."

Even you knew that something like that was about as smart as jamming a metal fork into an electrical outlet. This had the potential of bringing down the whole house of cards and he had the nerve yesterday to blame you for all of this. If you see Nikko again, you think you're going to be very tempted to beat the living crap out of him.

You meant to say *when* you see him again.

The shit is all flying so fast and heavy now and your head feels like a prize-fighter's speed bag. You are a baseball player, not a thinker, and you are angry at yourself for not figuring that smoking all of that dope lately wasn't going to make you slow. Trying to figure out exactly what Nikko is going to do with Bo's wallet is eluding you.

"Let's call over there," you tell Dan. "It might not be too late to stop him. I'll call information for the number for the Grand Tropic. What's the area code for Vegas?"

Hale was trying to say something and you hear the phone change hands again.

"No, don't do it. We tried already from a different phone off campus than this one, you can't call from there for the same reason that Dan couldn't make the radio station call from his room. If something happens they would see that a call came from this phone."

"Did you get him?"

"He hadn't checked in yet."

"At least not under his name," Hale says.

"Or Richard Boyd's name," Dan adds.

Bing-fucking-o. That's what Nikko was going to do with Bo's wallet. He was going to bomb the hotel that he thought ripped him off. He'd make a Doomsday Club call after it was all too late and once the smoke settled the police would get a suspect named Richard Boyd, a.k.a Bo, a.k.a. Major Dick. It was going back to square one. He is using Bo to get rid of the blame from the deaths that occurred from trying to get rid of him in the first place.

If that was the case then he probably would check in under Bo's name or something close. The sneaky bastard was making a phony paper trail leading right up to the burnt out shell of the

Grand Tropic. You had to hand it to him, there was something brilliantly evil about it but you couldn't let it happen in your right mind. There were bound to be more bodies. Lots of them. You knew that Nikko thought he had figured out some way he thought he could pull it off.

In their own way, the firebombs you had set off already were, for all intents and purposes, untraceable. A nine-volt battery attached to a plastic jar filled with beans and water? If the acetylene was capable of vaporizing a human body then there had to be so little of your detonators left that the crime lab boys would be scratching their heads for years trying to figure it out.

Saying this had completely gone too far would have been the understatement of the century. In the past ten minutes, your life was starting to seem like the drag race scene in *Rebel Without a Cause*. That's who you were, some poor jerk about to eat the jagged rocks below. You could feel the fragile floor of despair weaken with every step across the carpet of your existence.

In the back of your mind you can feel a toke craving coming on but you shove it out of your head. It's all the dope that had gotten your ass in this whole damn mess to begin with. If you hadn't been too busy drowning your sorrows in bongwater, you never would have been in the room when Bo showed up in the first place and you never would have swung the bat and so on and so on. So what if Dan got his ass beat up? You should have been in Fluid Dynamics and the whole goddamned mess wouldn't have been a single bit of skin off your ass. You could say the pot was responsible for what happened but that would be total bullshit, a complete and utter cop-out of biblical proportions. You might just as well blame the damn bat for Bo's death.

You are all responsible for all of the stuff that had gone down so far. Perhaps in the long run Nikko would have started blowing shit up on his own anyway even without having Bo to get rid of. He just had too much of that need in him wrapped up a little too tightly to begin with and it would have come out sooner or later in a big boom. He used to talk about what a liquored-up pusbag his pop was and your guess is that Nikko must have spent most of his life pretty well acquainted with the back of the old man's hand.

Probably a wickedly acute case of Hale's small dick syndrome theory in action since the apple doesn't fall too damn far from the tree. Nikko was treating the world the same way his pop treated him. Maybe he came from a long line of pyromaniacs and psychopaths. Whatever it was, it was obvious now that old Nikko should have been picked in high school as *Most Likely to be a Fucking Loony Toon.*

You're a ball player not a social worker, dammit. Maybe if you had come here on a poetry scholarship all of this shit never would have happened. On second guess, if you had come here on a poetry scholarship, someone probably would have beaten you to death by now instead.

"He might not have gotten there yet," you say to Hale. "He could still be on the highway. He could be planning to stay at any hotel under any name."

"Nah, he's going to stay at the Grand Tropic," Hale corrects you. "He needs a bathroom for his little gizmo so why not use a room at the hotel. You could set it up and walk out of there and let the whole thing blow eight hours later. He could be back here, standing in the middle of campus and have a thousand people see him here at the same time it goes off."

"Right, and if they ever trace where it went off it'll all lead to a room paid for with Bo's credit card."

It's funny, but sometimes your brain just knows to file away the tiniest fragment of information in case it becomes useful later. The voice you hear in your head sounds exactly the same coming out of Hale's mouth three days ago, just as the old melon had put it away for safe keeping.

I never realized this before, Nikko, but you and Bo could almost pass for brothers.

Wow, that was it all right. He really didn't look too much like Bo if you took into account the difference in height and bulk but would anyone remember that? Who knows?

The little voice in your head was screaming again for you to do something. Something to stop Nikko or the bomb. But what?

You had managed to get away with everything so far and Nikko's stunt brought incredible exposure. You'd have to face your maker someday with a shitload of explaining to do about the pile of bodies you left behind but that didn't seem to scare you as much as having to face the needle. The fact that somehow all those people had gotten killed made you positively sick inside but the more you thought about it, the more it seemed to melt away from your conscious guilt and turn more into something you saw rather than something you did. Your entire brain had washed itself into believing that it didn't have to take any responsibility for any of that. You'd cope with it later but now you had to just get yourself through the present. The here and now, baby steps to the front door, gotta walk before you can run.

"Look," Hale says. "We're going to drive out to another pay phone away from here and keep trying to call him at the Grand Tropic every fifteen minutes for the next hour or so. Just hang there and wait for us, I'll buzz you if we get in touch with him."

He doesn't even wait for an answer. Click. He is gone.

You are now stuck here in Purgatory until further notice. Although you hadn't thought of doing anything else you now want like hell to get out of this room and be anywhere but here. Out of the corner of your eye, you spot Hale's bong on the floor and it now has your full attention. It commands your eyes to lock onto it hypnotically while sweetly calling out to you.

Scott, Scott, you know you want me. Come and wrap your lips around me. Spark me up. I won't disappoint you. I'll make you happy.

You feel drawn to it like a moth to a flame and you know there's no way you could stick around here for a couple of hours on a Saturday afternoon without eventually finding yourself giving in. The flesh is willing and oh so incredibly weak.

Jackie's voice keeps filling your head as you bend over to pick up the bong. Not the *I wouldn't piss on you if you were on fire* voice but the sweet, soft way she would say something as you held each other after making love or the way she'd whisper dirty thoughts into your ear in the dark at Willington. It was seductive and you are in no kind of emotional state to resist. A thought hits you. You go to Hale's desk to find the hash that Snatch had sold him and it's gone.

"Damn!" You are pissed that he smoked it without you. And here you were about to steal it from him anyway.

No big deal, there is still some Mexican Brown left, not much, but enough to kill a couple of hours all by your lonesome.

You pack the bowl with Snatch's cheap weed and it occurs to you that next to the Thai stick you had gotten from Tom, this stuff looks like it had come out of the back end of a dog. You are looking for a lighter when your phone rings again. You pick it up, guessing it has to be Hale or Dan with some news, but it's not.

ONE6ix

"Scott, I need your help," the voice on the other end of the phone tells you. It sounds sincere and for a moment you almost buy it too.

"Fuck you, Nikko." You are angry. Correction, way pissed. You need to talk to him but all you want to do is scream. The blood inside of your veins just boils at the sound of his voice. If he had come through the door instead of just calling you probably would have thrown him through the wall. "What the hell do you think you're doing, you stupid asshole?"

"Scott, I'm serious. I went to Vegas to do something crazy and it's all kind of gone wrong. I can't say what over the phone but you've got to help me or we're all fucked!"

This has to take the cake. You should have locked him in the mop closet at Chicky's. Somehow you manage to push your anger aside to try and figure out what the hell has happened. There'd be plenty of time to kick his scrawny ass later.

"Look Nikko, I know where you are, just tell me what's going on."

"I can't say on the phone. Scott, you've got to get out here and hurry or the whole thing's blown for sure."

"What do you mean get out there? You said you're in Vegas, that's five hours away."

"Yeah, I am, but you can get here in a couple of hours if you take a plane. They have shuttles from LAX to Vegas every half hour. Take a cab to the Grand Tropic, it's on the strip, it's one of the older looking ones. Just tell the cabby to take you to the Grand Tropic. I'm in room 226. You got that?"

"Yeah, I got it." You write it down on the back of your copy of Nikko's runaway note.

"Room two twenty-six. Don't pack anything, don't bring anything just go! You gotta leave now! Okay?"

"Okay, okay," you impatiently tell him. Then a thought hits you almost too late. "What about Hale and Dan? They're out trying to reach you from a pay phone."

"Look, don't worry about them, that's why I called you. We all can't be seen here but you and I can just sneak out without anyone noticing, just like yesterday. The more people involved, the more danger there is. Just come by yourself."

"I gotta tell Hale something."

"Fine, leave him a note. Go get a piece of paper and a pen."

You resent the fact that he doesn't think that you can write a note but now isn't the time to argue. You reach into your desk to get a clean sheet of paper.

"Okay, go."

"Just write this. Hale, comma..."

You write it. Man, was he making you feel stupid.

"Got it."

"Bo needs your help."

"What? Are you crazy?" You look at Detective Martinez's card still on your desk. "I can't say that."

"Scott, chill out, nobody's going to see the damn note before Hale does. Fine, just write this... Had to go to fix a problem, will call you when I get there."

"Fine, whatever," you say as you write it down.

"Good, whatever you do, just don't put your name on it. You'll explain it to them later but now you have to get to the airport."

"Okay, okay."

"Scott, hurry please," he says and just hangs up. Doesn't anybody say goodbye anymore?

You're so mad you want to just smash your phone against the wall. Your mind was made up. When you got to Vegas, you'd help Nikko out of whatever fuckaboo he had gotten you all into and when it was all over you were going to smack him so hard even the monkeys he evolved from were going to feel it.

You stare at what you have written. How stupid. You feel like re-writing it but you don't want to take the time. Instead you take out another blank sheet of paper. You have another note to write.

Closing the door behind you, you do your usual check for your wallet and keys. Strangely enough, you always find yourself doing this *after* instead of before you've already shut the door. You walk down to Manny's room and slide the note you have just written under her door and turn to leave.

Almost instantly her door swings open. She is standing there in her sweats looking more than just a tad bit hungover.

"What gives?"

Even without any makeup on she looks pretty fabulous. There's just something about a woman who looks great without any makeup that just blows you away. Jackie was almost like that. When she'd go and put some on, you'd see a big difference. Not like night and day, she wasn't a sea hag or anything but just a little bit of lipstick and eye liner made the difference between boner with a big *B* or little *b*. The big secret was that she really knew how to put it on.

Some girls you've known just pile it on like the way you'd spackle an old wall, just tons and tons of base and blush and shadow and crap. Oh, and lip liner. If there's one thing you hated about Jackie's makeup scheme was that godawful lip liner.

But Manny, she'd look great in the middle of a hurricane. Just looking at her you can't even begin to tell her how sorry you are that you are going to have to miss your date.

"I thought you may be sleeping, you know, recuperating after a wicked night of scorpion bowling," you say.

"I was, well, kind of. Actually I was trying to decide what to wear to the party tonight."

Oh God. Why me? you think.

"Look, something kind of came up. A buddy of mine needs me to do some shit for him, and I forgot that I promised him a couple of weeks ago, and I'm afraid I might get stuck there."

That comes out bad. It's more than obvious by the look on her face that she isn't buying this one bit.

"I understand," she says flatly. She doesn't. The way it comes out of her mouth sounds like she means to call you an asshole but is too polite to do so.

"Sorry," you tell her. You are sorrier than you can imagine.

You think she's going to just turn around and shut the door in your face but she surprises you when she opens her mouth again.

"It's your ex-girlfriend, isn't it?"

You are almost relieved because nothing could be further from the truth.

"No, no," you say. "This has nothing to do with my ex or with any other girl for that matter." You don't want to say anything else but sometimes you just get going and the floodgates spill. "Look, to be perfectly honest with you, there's nothing else I'd rather do tonight than hang out with you and go to that party and get to know you better and finally kiss you and whatever."

You can't stop. From the smile on Manny's face you can tell she finds this all very amusing, and flattering.

"I mean," you keep going. "I really want to go out with you. The honest-to-God truth is a buddy of mine got into some kind of mess and... and I'm the only one who can help him and I know it sounds stupid, but I'm not sure exactly what's going on. I promise I'll try to explain it all when I get back."

You don't know how you're going manage to do that. You'll

cross that bridge when you get back, if it doesn't get blown up, that is.

"Look, don't worry about it," she says, and surprises you when she leans in to kiss you. After a second, you relax and as you open your lips you feel her tongue enter your mouth. It is a long, deep kiss that turns you to jello. She pulls back and gently wipes away the drool from your lip with the tip of her finger.

"Maybe if you don't get back too late you can just meet me there at the party or maybe here," she says, almost cooing. Inside your head you can hear a noise, a familiar one. *Ping.*

"I'll try to make it back as soon as possible. I promise."

Her smile is magnetic and you can't break away until she disappears back into her room.

"Wow," you say to yourself, shaking the cobwebs out of your head as you run for your car.

Saturday traffic in L.A. is usually as bad on the weekends as it is during the week but today everything is moving. Somehow luck finds you, if only just for a moment. You get to the airport quickly and park in short term. Desert Air has a small counter stuck in the corner with all of the other micro-airlines. You get in line behind a bunch of old people who look like they can't wait to go off and lose their pension money.

When you get to the window you buy a one-way ticket on the two o'clock which means you have five minutes to get on the plane. You start to feel all squirmy again. Your folks would never buy why ninety bucks for this ticket showed up on the emergency Visa bill so you consider just telling them the truth. That you did it to keep a friend from killing a whole shitpile of people. You think about it again and decide to pay cash instead.

You make the plane with plenty of time to spare and find an empty row near the back. You don't even want to think about Nikko or Vegas or any of that stuff. You want to think about the kiss, about Manny. Your thoughts race at a mile a minute and once the plane gets in the air, you doze off like a baby.

The waitress wakes you as the plane lands. You thank her and run through the terminal to grab a cab, making one quick stop.

Riding in the back of a taxi through Las Vegas is like getting a chance to see the world in a fishbowl. You see kids everywhere—kids clinging to their mother's dresses, kids in strollers, kids in diapers. For a moment you think you're at Disneyland. You've never liked Vegas at all. You kind of despise it. This is your third time here and right away you hate it more than the last time. You thought you'd never see this shithole again.

Your first time here was on a road trip your sophomore year with this pimply guy named Mason who was your freshman roommate the year before. You couldn't stand the guy but after not having to live with him you kind of missed the whiny bastard and became pretty decent friends until he transferred to some stupid school back east. Anyway, it was right as you started seeing Jackie, before the two of you got all hot and heavy. You and Mason did an overnight road trip to see Sin City. Boys night out. Although a few hours in the car listening to him piss and moan about some stupid term paper and watching him pick at his zits made you remember why you didn't want to room with him anymore.

The second time was when you came here with Jackie for a couple of days and you got to see a side of her you wished you hadn't. You were both too poor to gamble but did anyway. You were the big puss and stopped after dropping fifty bucks at the quarter slots. You expected to lose but Jackie acted like the casino owed it to her to let her win, that they had a lot of nerve taking what little money she had to lose. This, you would come to learn, was the prototypical Jackie view of life. The whole thing passed so quickly that it was hardly noticeable. You did though and afterwards you made sure the two of you spent most of the rest of the weekend in your room. Maybe that's why you hated Vegas so much. Today, you are here less than a half-hour and already you are itching to hightail it out of town at the first possible chance.

Saying the Grand Tropic is a throwback to the swinging Vegas of the fifties is just an incredibly polite way of calling it a total dump. The thing is a rundown eyesore desperately in need of a fresh coat of paint and barely qualified as being Downtown. It is a greasy little pimple on the dogbitten ass of this town.

You walk into the lobby and are fairly surprised to find it a bit nicer on the inside than you expected. Not too terribly nice, but nice in a walls covered with mirrors kind of way, if there is such a thing. The entrance to the tiny casino is over to one side but you don't really care too much since you just bee-line for the elevator.

Like most of the clientele, a lot of the places that haven't been rebuilt yet are pretty old, which in Vegas terms means like, thirty years or something. These are places filled with the cigar smoke and cheap perfume from decades when it was actually okay to buy both of those things from the same store. Today, mildew is most of what you smell in the second floor hallway when the elevator doors open—the smell of a place that has never *not* been air conditioned. You figure there still aren't a whole lot of windows that open in this town, especially once you get off of the ground floor. You are hoping that Nikko's room is close because you aren't in the mood to go traipsing around and bumping into the same people who you are probably just going to get killed. You fight off the passing thought of hoping Nikko has some doobage on him.

Luckily the room is close. Fifty rooms on a floor and two-two-six is to the right of the elevators. You stand at the door for a moment and stare at the carpet instead of knocking. It's kind of a pukey red with these trippy yellow *fleur-de-lys* all over it. You had seen shit like this in every cheap, shitty motel that Jackie and you had ever stayed in. You know your mind is on the not well side of reality when you see a bad carpet and all you think about is your ex.

Even in the face of complete panic and possible ruination of your life as you know it, you are still fixated on someone who thinks of you as no more than a bad joke. You can hear Nikko talking to somebody and you begin hoping maybe Hale has finally gotten a hold of him and is busy knocking some sense into that thick poindexter skull of his. Anything to make getting the hell out of here easier. There is every reason for you to believe that whatever is going to happen from this point forth was going to be one hell of a mess.

You have already forgotten how much you wanted to kick Nikko's scrawny ass earlier. Something about this whole thing makes you more nervous than a long-tailed cat in a room full of rocking chairs. As atheists go, you consider yourself Orthodox, but right now you begin asking God to get your dumb ass out of this mess.

I swear to fly my shit straight from now on, you think to yourself before realizing that the big G probably didn't take too kindly to profanity in the suggestion box. Oh well, another prayer left unanswered, take your complaint to the customer service window.

You have very little clue what exactly to expect when you knock on the door to room 226. To say that your balls leap into your throat when Hale answers the door would be a major understatement.

ONE7

One time, your parents threw a surprise party on your ninth birthday, and once on a Christmas break, Jackie took you to the rec room at your parents' condo complex and peeled off a sweater and peasant skirt to show off the hot lingerie she had put on underneath. Both times you would have been able to drive a semi into your open mouth. But now, standing in the hall looking at Hale smiling at you like that, you could have taken that truck and done a three-point turn in it.

"Hey buddy, come on in, take off your skin and rattle around in your bones," he says. It's obvious you appear too stunned for words, so he puts his hand on your shoulder and kind of guides you over the threshold. He does it a way that makes you think if you really did faint, he'd just grab you by the scruff of the neck to keep you on your feet.

Of the three other people in the room you are fairly well acquainted with two, having spent the better part of the last few days smoking dope in your room with them. The guy wearing only his underwear on the bed however, lying face up, with his hands and feet bound by clothesline and a strip of duct tape across his mouth—you have no fucking clue who he is. The first thought in your now-jumpy mind was that it's Bo. Of course it isn't though, this guy is big like Bo but the comparison ends there. You notice a big wet spot underneath his ass on the cheap blue bedspread. His eyes are bugging out trying to get a good look at you and your guess is that he may have first thought you were the cavalry before finally realizing that were only just another bug who had fallen into the venus fly trap.

Hale reaches over with a thumb on your chin and pushes your mouth closed.

"You look like a fucking retard standing there with your yap open like that," he says to you.

Dan and Nikko stand there behind Hale, obviously finding this all pretty funny. Your balls are giving you a bad feeling about this. Whatever is going on here feels like some kind of bad dream. That's it, you are still on the plane asleep in your seat, having a really bad nightmare of some kind or maybe this is all some sort of bad pot trip. That had to be it. The vibe you get is all wrong, it has to be a hallucination. Regardless of whether this is the dope or the four bad tacos from lunch talking, you are going to bug out of this wacky dream room before the walls start singing Barney songs or something. If anytime is a good time to wake up, this is surely it. You think of Hale's voice this morning talking about your futures, and penance, and solving the problem and it all clicks into place what this little pow-wow is all about.

Social Darwinism. Survival of the fittest. For a weird second you try to remember what happened at the end of *Lord of the Flies*.

You take a look over your shoulder at the door, which telegraphs your idea to make a run for it. It all still feels like some sort of trance until Hale's hand on your shoulder again startles you.

He puts his face just inches from yours. "Uh, uh."

There is no doubt in your mind that you are stronger than him. You're an athlete, well sort of an athlete, and the most exercise that he ever got regularly was getting up to fill his bong with water. If you threw, you were very sure you'd be treating him to a fresh, frosty helping of whup-ass. Hell, you could take Hale and Fuckin' Dan too if it came down to that, which you are hoping it doesn't. Since the guy on the bed didn't look like he'd put up much of a fight, you are pretty sure there'd be plenty to go around.

You are getting pretty sick of being touched all the time by everybody and the immediate thought of that blows the fog from your brain. There is something rotten in Denmark and you have to make a break for it. Time to blow town starting with this room. Nikko is still smiling and it hits you where you had seen that look before—on Bo's face when he thought that he had busted you good. It is a total *your ass is grass* look. You do the very first thing that comes to mind, you smile back. First at Nikko and then at Hale.

In the blink of an eye you reach over, grab Hale's wrist from your shoulder, and the look on his face changes from *catbird seat* to *crap your pants* shock. With everything you've got, you slam your elbow into his side and snap it back quickly to get him again before he knows what's happening. He tries to squirm out of your grip and turns slightly so the second shot connects more under his arm and you hear a wet crack when it hits. Your first thought is that your elbow has broken and you're in that extremely brief interim before a sickening wave of nausea and pain would rocket up your arm like a tsunami. You realize quickly though when Hale falls to the floor like someone has pulled his feet out from under him it isn't your elbow that busted, it's one of his ribs.

At first, you are horrified that you've hurt him so badly. You remember there was this time when you were all living in the

Towers that he had sprained his ankle jumping off of a bunk stoned and cried like a baby about it for days. It was the only extended period of time where he had lost his calm that anyone knew of. You knew that he was a puss about pain and seeing him lying there curled up in the fetal position on the floor, you figured he must be dying. The moment's pause to look at him on the floor was enough to let Dan grab a hold of you.

The jump you had gotten on Hale had startled Nikko and Dan too much to move a muscle. If you had just kept moving and booked out of the room you might have made it to the elevator before they could have even batted an eyelash or said *boo*.

What stops you isn't a physical force of any kind but something from inside of you. A feeling from your balls telling you not to run, not to move and not to even breathe funny because they knew before you did that pointed at your head was some type of gun.

"Hold your ass right the fuck there Scott," Dan's voice tones out coldly from behind you.

You only see it out of the corner of your eye at first but hearing the dry click of the hammer being pulled back is enough to convince you that your balls are absolutely right. He jams the gun into your face and as you turn around very carefully, the barrel pushes up against your cheek hard enough that you think he is going to push it right through your cheek into your mouth or break half of your back teeth. He uses his other hand to grab a great big handful of your shirt to keep you from going anywhere, not that you have any intention to. Your only thoughts are that, to all appearances, you are probably only a short breath or two away from getting a 45 caliber facelift.

Very carefully, Hale gets up off of the floor. It is obvious as he makes it to his feet that he's in extreme pain and he gingerly puts one hand just under his arm where you hit him. What strikes you even more than that is his face and the wetness that rolls down his cheek. His eyes glare at you like a pair of red-hot laser beams.

You watch as he takes a step towards you and holds his hand out to Dan.

"Gun," he says.

Dan looks at you, then at Hale and reluctantly hands him the piece. Taking it in his trembling hands he points it right at your face. You think he might actually pull the trigger.

"Somebody's going to hear that if it goes off," Dan says nervously. "If you shoot him, we're all fucked."

You think you're a goner for sure. In your mind, getting splattered all over the wall of a shithole like this is not your choice of how you want to spend the rest of your Saturday afternoon. You hurt him badly. You can't take your eyes off of how his hand shakes as he brings the gun up to your face. You want to look away but can't bring yourself to.

All you can think of is the last thing you'd ever see if you were shot in the face, in the instant before the eternal darkness rushed in, would be the flash of the muzzle and then you'd be turned off like someone hit a lightswitch. You can feel your heart galloping in your mouth. You shift your eyes to Nikko's and in that moment Hale nods his head before bringing the gun back with one quick move.

You see the gun coming fast, and as it hits you in the jaw, you are surprised at how hard he had connected. Falling to your knees on the floor, you can feel the warm salty taste of blood in your mouth. The inside of your cheek has gashed up against your teeth and you can feel with the side of your tongue that it was starting to swell up immediately. Catching your breath, you lean forward a little and spit out a long gooey strand of blood and saliva onto the crummy hotel room carpet. You watch it hang out of your mouth and hit the floor, and to your mild surprise, discover none of your dental work has come out into the gross and tiny puddle you have made there. You think it's a miracle that the gun didn't go off when he hit you with it.

"Get up, Scott," you hear Hale say. His voice sounds strained as if he were pinned under a boulder.

You pretend like you don't even hear him. You know they wouldn't dare pull the trigger unless they had to, so you stay on the floor.

Before Hale has a chance to say it again, Dan grabs a handful of your collar and yanks you up to your feet. At no time had you ever thought he was that strong but he lifts you up like you were just a sack of potatoes, like you were nothing to him. It's obvious that helping all of those kids move with his truck was putting some muscle on him. You might have underestimated old Dan but the fact that Nikko didn't move at all when you were hitting Hale makes you think you could easily take him if you got the jump. If you really had to.

Dan pushes you across the room towards the bed. You look at the guy lying there all tied up in his underwear and you still can't guess who in the hell this poor schlub is. His eyes are locked on you. You don't know how scared you look to this guy but he stares at you like you're a dead man.

"Get on the bed, Scott. Don't make this any more fuckin' difficult than it has to be, for God's sake," Dan tells you. He means it too. You'd think you were going to make him late for a big date or something, like it was going to be your fault.

You sit on the edge of the bed and look at those guys, your so-called friends. In your mind you are still trying to put all of the pieces together and the puzzle isn't looking right, no way brother, no goddamned way. The way things appear, you are about to become the recipient of the very short end of the stick.

"What the hell is going on here?" you ask. Nobody answers. You turn to your roommate. "Hale?"

He motions at you with the gun. You think of saying something else but figure right now, diplomacy was going to be the art of saying *nice doggie* until you could back up far enough to find yourself a good sharp rock.

"Scott, lie down."

For a moment you think of making another rush at him but what chance would you stand with him having a gun? You do as he says. In the movies, the guy with the piece pointed at him always makes a last ditch play for the gun instead of lying down like a lamb and you start thinking that seeing one pointed at you for real, not on TV or in the movies, has cured you of any kind of ridiculous hero complex. You know if you made a move for him or the gun, he'd have to pull the trigger, sure and simple. You start to think if you let them tie you up like the other guy there might be a better chance later than making a desperate charge at a loaded pistol. The way things are looking, you don't really have a choice. You lay down on the bed.

Right away, Dan starts tying your hands behind you with clothesline and it seems like he knows what he's doing because it's going on thick. Nikko reaches into his knapsack and pulls out a roll of grey duct tape, rips off a piece and plasters it across your mouth. He kind of looks at you, tilts his head to the side and just shrugs his shoulders. You had seen him do that same move a thousand times, as if to say *oops, hey, sorry* when he really wasn't too sorry to begin with. Every time he'd spill a Coke on your crappy area rug he'd just shrug. You are sure of one thing. If and when the chance comes, you are definitely going to enjoy every second of kicking the living shit out of him.

After Dan ties your hands he does your feet the same way. It feels like your hands are a bit looser than you expected but you're afraid to check right now and arouse suspicion. You can tell you are lying in the puddle of the other guy's pee on the bed because you can smell it and it starts to seep through your jeans onto your leg. At this point you are more pissed off than worried about being pissed on. A little urine on your leg is going to be way on the bottom of your list of worries right now.

Hale comes over and sits on the edge of the bed next to you. "Well, buddy, I guess we owe you an explanation."

Fucking-A right you do, assfuck, you try to say with your eyes.

"See, we have a problem, a pretty big fucking problem here and you, my friend, are the reason that we have it. You see, it's not so much that you killed Bo. That was a very unfortunate accident. If we had been able to get rid of the body the way we wanted to in the first fire we wouldn't be having this little conversation right now. The big fucking problem here is that we've managed to kill a fuckload of people through another series of unfortunate accidents. Do you think the cops are ever going to stop looking for the fucking Doomsday Club? Do you think the government is going to stop hunting for us? Somehow I really don't fucking think so! They're going to turn over every fucking rock, every fucking leaf and look under every fucking dog turd in the city until they come up with something. Now we're as far as we can be from any kind of heat right now, and as long as any of us doesn't do anything completely stupid we're going to skate.

"This is where you come in, Scott," he says, waving the gun at your chest. "The three of us don't think you can keep from blowing the whole deal for all of us. Now, I know that you're not so dumb as to do it intentionally but somewhere along the line you're going to accidentally open your yap and say something to somebody like that new girlfriend of yours, that Manny chick. Or, what I'm really afraid of is that you're so fucking emotionally unstable right now over that dumb slut Mitten, that you're going to go all Three Mile Island on us and spill this whole mess to a shrink or a cop or your folks or write it in a journal where someone will find it. You see Scott, this has nothing to do with you. I like you, you're kind of a mope for the most part but you're kinda alright."

He takes a pause to look at you and says what you're expecting.

"But your unstable behavior is going to get us all sent to fucking death row and I can't have that, you stupid jackass!"

He gets up without saying anything else and sits down slowly in a chair and just stares out of the window holding his hand over his broken rib. You notice he winces when he swallows so he must be hurting but he keeps his poker face on in front of the boys.

Internal bleeding would really suck for you, shithead, you start thinking. The side of your face is throbbing.

Hale has the gun but this is a committee decision. Now that you were officially told the *why,* the *what* was pretty obvious. No one has explained the how yet, or the who as in *who is this guy whose piss you're lying in*? You should have known though even before Dan starts to explain.

"Scott, I came up with this idea that would finally clean the whole fucking slate and would make the cops think that Bo and the Doomsday Club are one and the same. They close the case and we're scott free from having to ever worry about it again. The problem is that it requires one more bomb and I didn't think you'd go for it or be able to pull it off without some kind of fucking panic attack."

There was something to that you suppose. It's true that you were feeling like everything was hanging by a very thin thread, especially after last night. The bomb, all those people getting killed and the way that Jackie acted like you were some kind of joke. You were screwing up your grades and most likely off the team for good, and anybody who would cut their own hair and leave it all hacked up for days was probably a complete nutter to begin with. It didn't take a clairvoyant to see where they were coming from. This was turning into some kind of half-assed intervention like if you were the alcoholic in the family or something. There was no denying that you had gone over the wall this past week. You were gone.

"It's nothing personal, really, it isn't," Hale says, looking at you and then over to Nikko and then out the window.

Nothing personal? Is he kidding? They're making like they're going to fucking kill you and it's nothing personal? It's a bad cliché, a goddamned cop out, of course it's personal. Next to using someone's toothbrush you'd pretty damn well say that taking their life qualifies for personal. Did they really think saying that made it easier for you? Something though is telling you none of these guys are going to lose too much sleep over this. They are enjoying it. It's all just another part of this big game they had created from the start.

"Now, Scott," Dan says. "We never introduced you here to your new friend. Scott, meet Bo. Bo, Scott," he gestures with his hand.

"Well, it's not really Bo, of course and I really don't give a flying fuck what his name is, but for simplicity sake let's just call him Mr. P. You see Mr. P. here is some kind of faggoty male prostitute that we picked up on the strip. Not that any of us are into that, you know Scott," he says with a wink. "It's just that we happened to notice that old Mr. P. here has a similar build to your old buddy, the late Major Dick. So, you see, we leave enough of him that when they find a bone fragment or two they'll think it's the same guy who the room is registered under, a Mr. Richard Boyd. USMC. Originally we were just going to burn you up as Bo but then we'd have to explain *your* disappearance and that'd just put us back to square one. This way we'll just make up some fucking thing about how you are some kind of *special friend* to Bo and he called you from Vegas saying he was in trouble, or to get married, or whatever."

It was all too clear where this was going. *Bo's special friend?* Bo calling you because he was in trouble? Who'd believe that? You'd be nuts to think that this was going to work. Or would you?

"Did you leave the note like I told you to?" Nikko asks.

You don't have to answer that question, he knows you did. You pulled out that piece of paper and let him dictate exactly what they wanted you to write. You try to remember what it said. Something ambiguous like *had to go help a friend*, but nothing that couldn't be construed as anything they wanted it to be. Christ, he had even tried to get you to write that you were going to see Bo in the first place. They really had set you up good. Hale and Dan's phony call when they were already here. Nikko's phone call from the room. The frame was fitting rather nicely.

Nikko starts in again. "You see, Scott, you and Bo are actually good friends but kept it secret for some reason or another and everybody will believe anything about you since you've become Psycho-boy now anyway. So, Bo calls you up on the phone to confess that he's this Doomsday Club thing and he's sorry that he killed all of these people and he didn't know who else to turn to so he called you and you came out. It's just that something went wrong and you two accidentally blew yourselves up in the room. I know it sounds completely farfetched now but if the cops blame Bo for the bombings and all of the people that were killed, then all we have to do is account for you and that's much easier."

If the Doomsday Club trail led to Bo, then case closed. Nikko,

Hale and Dan would be clean. Trying to explain why you got killed with him would be a better deal than sitting around waiting for you to screw it all up somehow. As a bonus, Nikko got to settle his stupid score with the Grand Tropic. In a twisted way, it made sense and that's the thing that made it all possible. Without a doubt in your mind, you now know for sure that there is no way you are all going to walk out of this room together.

"Oh Danny-boy," Nikko calls out even though he's only an arm's length away. "Let's get that phone number, I'd really like to get back in time for the Alpha Pi party."

Dan says nothing but picks up the phone book from the nightstand by the bed and drops it onto the table where Hale is sitting. Nikko keeps his stare on you for a moment longer, looking and squinting like he's trying to read your mind. You aren't sure of what he's going to do next so it spooks you a little. A little more of this and it was going to be your turn to wet yourself.

Nikko turns his attention to his knapsack and pulls out the roll of duct tape again. Slowly, he tears off a long strip. You can hear clearly as each little bit comes free. It reminds you of the sound of sucking.

"Well, Mr. P. I'll tell you what," he says with a cold grin plastered across his face. "I'll let you go if you answer one little question."

ONE8

Hale and Dan both look over as if they had been expecting something like this to happen but are still uncomfortable with it.

Mr. P. nods his head furiously, his eyes are so wide open that you're sure they're just going to shoot right out of his head and onto the floor.

"One question, got it?"

Mr. P. nods even faster.

"Okay, for what's behind door number one..." Nikko gestures at the way out of the room. "...answer this question."

The nodding gets faster still.

"Spell... *chrysanthemum.*"

You can hear Mr. P's. muffled voice through the tape and it doesn't matter what letter he tries to say because they all sound the same. Nikko hovers over him like a vulture, shaking his head, waiting for the inevitable. Mr. P. gets about three letters in and stops. You can tell he knows it's too late. Nikko slaps another strip of tape across his nose, completely blocking the only airway he has left.

It doesn't take long for Mr. P. to realize there isn't a damn thing he can do about his situation. He tries screaming his airways open anyway and when that doesn't work he starts kicking and bucking like a man having a seizure. From six inches away you can't help but actually smell the stink of fear coming off of him. You can't watch. You try turning onto your side because he starts to kick your legs in his effort to get free. You brace for the impact of his head smashing into yours and tuck your chin down as far as it will go without pressing on the swollen part too much.

Nikko turns the TV on, punching the volume up to cover the muffled screams. Mr. P's bucking becomes harder. He shakes the whole bed so much that you're afraid he's going to bounce you right onto the floor. In a way, you are really kind of hoping that he would so you won't have to be lying there next to him when he eventually dies. He tries one more big kick but he catches the back of your leg instead and ends up pitching himself off of the mattress and onto the floor. You can't see where he landed and you don't care since all you can think about is the exploding pain from where he kicked you. For a second you think he might have broken a bone or something. You wiggle your toes and the only pain you feel is in your calf where he connected.

You roll onto your back again and try to see where Mr. P. has gone to. Within seconds he begins convulsing and you feel him weakly kick one of the bed legs twice before he stops moving entirely.

The guys are all fixated on the body. You can tell nobody was expecting that. Nikko looks like a kid who's just seen his first circus.

"Well *that* was fucked up," Dan says, turning away from the body in disgust.

For some reason it strikes you as ironic that it's going to end the same way it started—four guys and a dead body in a room together. You guess it's true what they say—what goes around comes around.

"Time to make the donuts!" Nikko exclaims in a sickly fascinated way like a kid at Christmas. He walks over to your side of the bed and the way he moves reminds you of that creepy nazi dentist in *The Marathon Man*. The guy that was always asking Dustin Hoffman *is it safe?* Just thinking that sends a chill down your spine.

The white porcelain lamp on the bedside table is about two feet tall and looks solid. At the point Nikko begins sizing it up, you start to really get worried to the point of near panic. When he picks it up and unplugs it, a gruesome thought comes to mind.

He's going to smash my head open like a walnut with that thing. Unintentionally, you made a sound that is more than likely a scream muffled by the duct tape. You look over at Dan and Hale and they are still just sitting in their chairs over on the other side of the room. The way they just sit there is like they're just watching HBO or something.

"Relax buddy," Nikko says. "We're your friends. We're not going to hurt you." He shifts the weight of the lamp to cradle it in one arm and leans over to pat the tender bruise on your cheek a couple of times. "We're going to let the big boom-boom take care of that."

As he turns away, you can hear him chuckling to himself. Man, you are starting to really hate that stupid bastard.

Looking around the room first, he decides to carry the lamp

over to the table. Dan takes one look at the battered thing and pushes his chair away from the lamp like he's afraid to even be near it. Nikko just chuckles again. There is a nut that holds the dusty shade onto the lamp and once Nikko has that off he just frisbees the shade into the corner. Without it, the lamp seems naked and the shape of it is almost feminine.

Nikko fixates on it as if taking its hat off had transformed it into some sort of featureless and supine white porcelain Virgin Mary. He runs his hand along the curves of the base as if he was caressing it, frowning as he pulls his hand away to see the dust that has come off with it.

Without a word, he snatches his knapsack from off the carpet and rummages through it until he finds what he's looking for—a teaspoon. He breathes on it and rubs it on his shirt to clean it before showing it to you, turning it back and forth in his hand.

"Now, you know as well as I do after our last two experiments that it's damn near impossible to get a bean detonator to go off exactly when you want it to, so I decided to go with something a little more trustworthy."

Reaching into his bag again he pulls out something square, a plastic box you don't quite recognize at first.

"Ta-da!" Nikko brings it closer so you can see it clearly. "It's a lamp timer. Get it?"

You do start to get it as you watch him crack open the lightbulb and expose the intact heating element. This is the new detonator alright, new and improved.

"What do you think, guys? It's quarter to four now, lets set it for five."

He fiddles with the box to set up the times. At five o'clock the lamp would turn on, the element would heat up in a bathroom full of acetylene and this room would make a pizza oven look like a deep freeze. A hotel like this, put up before real building codes existed, was likely to turn into an inferno before the first fire truck even showed up. That would certainly keep them from cheating any other scam artists in the casino again for sure. You know if he had it his way, Nikko would have rather just found the arrogant pit boss who tossed him out and jammed the bomb right up his ass. Hey, if you had your way, you just might let him too instead of how this looked like it was all going to play out.

Balancing the weight of the lamp carefully he instructs Dan to bring the timer into the bathroom with him. You listen as they fiddle to set it up and wonder to yourself what he was expecting you to do for the next hour. Getting the lamp in place only takes a minute, and after that you hear the sound of ripping tape again as they make an attempt to cover the vent above the sink. You are able to run through a number of different scenarios in your mind of how this is all going to end, each one finishing with something less than happy. Before they come out again you hear someone turn on a faucet and the sound of a torrent of water rushing out to fill the bathtub.

Hale won't look back at you even though you try to catch his eye. Instead he just stares out the window, waiting for whatever is going to happen to just happen already. He puts the gun down on the table then reaches into his pocket and pulls out the little foil-wrapped square of hash that Snatch had sold him and a small bowl made out of marble that he had gotten down in T.J. years ago.

It was this funky grey thing that looked like it came off of a chessboard or something. Your guess is that some Mexican guy carved a bunch of chessmen and after nobody bought them he turned them into pipes to toke out of. Hale often joked about playing with a whole set like that and every time you captured a piece you got to smoke the whole bowl. You told him that you'd never finish the game because you'd eventually lose your desire to actually win.

"Ahhh, killer idea, man," Nikko says to Hale as he watches him get ready to toke. "Spark me."

He puts a little bit of the hash in the bowl and lights it up. You watch him shut his eyes as he sucks in the smoke. In all of the time you had known him he always toked with his eyes open. He always squinted around the room like he knew he was being a bad kid or something. It always cracked you up when he did that. You could tell he was nervous. The shit was about to go down and everybody was about to get their hands dirty one last time.

You watch him suck in the smoke and there's no part of you that wants any. You'd think a guy in your spot would be trading his soul for a last hurrah, one last toke before darkness but not you, not anymore. You make up your mind right there that you are quitting. Dope had gotten you in this whole mess to begin with and if you died now, you'd at least die clean.

After a couple of minutes, Hale stops holding his side, the hash is making him feel better. He pinches off a small bit from the unwrapped chunk of unsmoked dope on the table next to him and drops it in the bowl before handing it and the lighter off to Nikko. As Hale leans back in his chair you are surprised to see him give you a wink before looking out the window.

You shift your gaze towards Nikko as he lights up the bowl and fills his lungs with hash smoke. He is standing on the other side of the bed close to where Mr. P. is lying dead on the floor, pacing back and forth as he tokes. It's getting more and more obvious everyone is totally on edge.

Nikko holds the pipe up to you in a mock toast. "A friend with hash," he says.

"Will burn your ass," Dan finishes, pointing right back at him. Nikko finds this hilarious and reaches over to give him a high-five. Very pleased with the fact he had made a funny, Dan lifts his palm to receive it. You catch a brief glance at the gun still sitting on the table.

The other guys don't even look at you, but Nikko, he is on fire now. He starts talking to you because you are the guest of honor at The Doomsday Club wrap party. He keeps pacing back and forth. There is something else to share with you before they leave you.

"You know, Scott, I had this great idea in the car on the way from L.A. that I told these guys and now I'm going to tell you." You catch a glimpse of Hale and Dan and they are shifting uncomfortably in their seats, obviously not really in the mood to listen to this again. "I was watching CNN at my parent's house over the holidays they said all of those retail stores in the malls, you know like KB Toys and Waldenbooks do something like thirty percent of their entire yearly sales total in the month of December? Isn't that amazing? Huh?"

Nikko waits for you to acknowledge this so you nod.

"They said since sales were down a couple of percent across the board this past year that we'd all feel the effects of it in a few months. Can you believe that? What a goddamn scam. You have to spend more money at Christmas so that the whole economy doesn't shit the bed."

You nod again, figuring you might as well go along with it.

"So, I started thinking, what if nobody went into the malls during the holidays? Nobody. All of these stores would go out of business and it would certainly do a number on the entire economy, right? Right? Now, what if, and this is a big what if, you are to go into a mall, say a really big one right at high noon on the day after Thanksgiving. Say at twelve sharp you walk into the food court. Have you ever been to a mall food court during the holidays? It's a goddamned zoo! People pushing, people shoving, you get to see some real nice fucking holiday spirit in a mall, oh boy, and how, brother. So what if you are to walk into the food court carrying a shopping bag from Sneaker Barn and in that bag was a shoe box with ten pounds of plastic explosive hooked to a five minute timer. You could just walk into a food court and drop that into a trashcan in the middle of zillions of people and nobody would think twice about it."

Man, this has the stink of something godawful already but you just keep on nodding your head. You just need to buy more time.

"So, you put a little box of goodies in a trash can and turn around and walk to an exit and leave. Ahh, but on your way out you drop another bomb in a trashcan by the door, but this one's on a seven minute timer and it's filled with nails and glass and shit like that. So, you get it? The first one goes off in the food court, but the second one, that's the money bomb. That one goes off as everyone is running like hell to get out of there. You have to admit, it's pretty damn sick but it's brilliant."

Obviously from the way he is nodding, he is in complete

agreement with himself. It is hypnotic in a way and you find yourself nodding along with him in the same rhythm, both of you just staring and nodding at each other like a couple of idiotic figures in a Bavarian clock or something.

"Now, what you do is you pull this little stunt in three big malls across the country at the very same time so nobody thinks anybody copycatted the first one. You do three big malls at the very same time and then you let the network news know that it was the Doomsday Club and that you're pissed that Christmas has been turned into this big plastic joke and until everybody can learn the true lesson of love and kindness and peace and joy and all that crap, that they better stay the hell out of the malls because you're going to be watching. So, nobody goes into the malls and the entire American economy goes into the toilet. Isn't it great?"

By the time he finishes, you are thoroughly stunned. He is going to teach the world peace and love by bombing the hell out of it, by burning it to the ground. Any shred of a valid point is all twisted and obscured by this hateful megalomania. Sometime in the previous twenty-four hours you began to realize you are Pandora and Nikko is the Box. If there had been any lingering doubt about it before, there certainly isn't any now.

"You know," Nikko says, leaning closer to you. "It's kind of a shame to put this whole Doomsday Club thing to bed." He looks at you and winks. "But, like they say. All good things... boom-boom, Scott. Boom-boom."

He reaches into his bag one last time and, to your surprise, out come three gallon-size ziploc bags, each filled with carbide. Instantly your head becomes awash with calculations. The last two bombs were each made with less carbide than half what was in one of these bags. Six times that was going to create an explosion big enough to do God knows what. Now you realize why they needed the bathtub. There is no doubt in your mind that when five o'clock comes around, the Grand Tropic was going to once again be the hottest place in town.

ONE9

Instead of just dumping all three bags of carbide into the tub, Nikko slits their sides and tosses them in so they'd dissolve slower. Standing a couple of careful steps away he waits and watches as the water turns grey and fizzes lightly from the chemical reaction. The acetylene gas starts to form. There'd be enough of it in the room by five o'clock to make this the biggest show this town has ever seen.

Nikko reaches back and pulls the bathroom door shut behind him. The timer was set, the lamp was ready and the juice was bubbling in the tub. There was only one thing left to do.

"Ready to make that call, Danny-boy?"

Dan smiles at him uncomfortably. Obviously putting up with it since it was turning into appease the lunatic hour. Getting up from his chair, he closes the phone book and doesn't even glance at you as he walks over to the bed to pick up the phone. Judging from the strained look on his face, you don't think he could have managed to look at you without saying more than he should have, even if he wanted to. You can tell by the fitful shuffling of feet and bodies that the tension in the room is starting to get to everybody. Every soul amongst the four of you is fully aware that there is a bomb brewing in the next room over and the quicker this was all taken care of, the better at this point.

Hale returns to holding the gun in the hand he isn't using to hold over his cracked rib. After the call, it was adios. This is endgame alright and your heart pounds like an earthquake.

The plan they had made together gave them a great opportunity to get out of town. This time though, instead of calling in with the exact location of the bomb, they'd just say that it was somewhere downtown. Now, of all of the hotels here, who'd suspect this crappy one right? The police would have to evacuate every hotel in town and there'd be catastrophic panic. Human nature being what it is, they were betting people would be trampling their own mothers to get out of town once that happened. All the boys would have to do at that point would be to slip out just slightly ahead of the crowd.

By the time the cops would be notified they'd have less than an hour and they'd be too busy getting people to safety to even look for the bomb. When all was said and done, after they finished piecing all of the bits together days or weeks from now, it was all going to point to Bo and his special friend, Scott Lorlon. You imagined that Jackie would probably be right in there with all of her dipshit pals in their *told ya's*.

Before this week, your life had pretty much been alright. Christ, even more than alright and you were just a big downer waiting to happen, pissing off everyone in the balance. Now you were bound and gagged in a cheap crappy hotel that was about to become a gigantic clambake, there's a dead half-naked male prostitute on the floor, the inside of your mouth is still bleeding and you've pretty much lost the feeling in your feet from having them tied.

This is what your life has come to. One incredibly fucked up week beyond the possible realm of human belief. You think a guy in your position would have his entire life flash before his eyes. Here you are lying on the lumpy bed with some stranger's piss still soaking into the leg of your jeans, looking at the ten-year-old pastel striped wallpaper and all you can manage is having the last few days flash before your eyes. In its own turgid litany of bullshit and presumption, the last few days had assumed the form of an entirely different life from the one that was there before. It is a horrid version of being born again for a soul too incredibly blind and irresponsible to realize that he had been born right the first time.

However, your mind parks on one thing from this past week. The one good thing.

Amanda.

You hardly knew Manny at all but there was something about her that you had felt enter the core of your very soul. It captured your fancy and danced through your thoughts. The way she laughed at you, the way she smiled. It was a tenderness that went far beyond a physical attraction—it was a chemistry. Enough chemistry to make an atom bomb look like a beer fart. Cupid's arrow had struck hard and only now were you realizing it. There was something about your relationship with Jackie that you'd been lying to yourself about all along. It was obvious from the way she treated you that she never really loved you. Sure she said it, hell, you told each other all of the time but you know what? You feel like a real class-A dick now because when you said it, you meant it. When she said it, it was because she liked the way it sounded. She never really loved you, she just loved the idea of being in love. Truth of the matter was that she wouldn't know what love was if it came in her mouth and told her it'd call her next week.

Amanda was different though. You had a date tonight with the one person so far in your life who had the potential to be *the one*. Instead you were tied to a bed in Vegas playing the part of the human sacrifice in your own personal episode of *The Twilight Zone*. This is what your life has come to.

Needless to say, you aren't too happy with it.

You watch Dan punch the numbers into the phone. Nikko is busy packing up his little bag of tricks and when he sees you watching him, he just smiles and shoots you your gang hand sign.

Yeah, shove that up your ass, you think.

With all of the numbers dialed except one, Dan pauses and looks over his shoulder at Nikko.

"Hey, you want to read the threat? My mouth is awful dry and I don't feel like going into the can to get a glass of water."

Nikko's face lights up and his expression just screams *gimme, gimme, gimme*. He sees you watching him and a big smile comes over his face.

"Tell you what Scott, since we go way back, after I get off of the phone, I'll give you a choice. The duct tape or the bomb."

Some choice.

Nikko nods and Dan punches in the last number and it starts to ring. He holds up one finger as he waits for someone to pick up and Nikko bobs up and down, biting his lip, just juiced to take the phone. A moment later Dan hands him the receiver and the piece of paper with the threat written on it. Nikko takes both and reads it word for word.

"This is the Doomsday Club. After our last target we have found even greater greed, larceny and selfishness than there is in Beverly Hills."

He tries to sound very angry to get the point across. Honestly, you don't think much of it is an embellishment.

"We came to the desert to let the earth now reclaim a past mistake and to appease an angry and vengeful God. There is a bomb in a hotel Downtown in Las Vegas. You have one hour to find it. Remember what happened yesterday. We are very, very serious."

After reading this last line he looks over at you and the guys and shoots the hand sign again. He is just absolutely beaming. It was a hundred Christmas mornings rolled into one and it is obvious that this is the biggest moment of his life. There is one last line that he reads. It is the same as from the note yesterday.

"Do you understand?"

If he had tried to hang up quicker, Nikko never would have heard the voice on the other end of the phone. He hung on though because he wanted to hear the fear in their trembling response. It was a real longshot but you had counted on this from the beginning. You knew that once he realized what number had been dialed, you'd have the jump on him.

"Sir, this is the 911 operator, I'm putting you straight through to the police."

The utter shock and realization on Nikko's face is immediate. He fucked up. His voice had been recorded, every bit of it and the cops are most likely on their way right now. Most of the circuitry in his brain doesn't want to believe it. How could it be? He is smart enough to understand though. He's been tricked. The bolt of lightning fires through his synapses, and you have tricked him.

Never in his life has Nikko ever thought he'd end up on the losing side of Social Darwinism. It was survival of the fittest alright and you had him beat. You remember hearing stories once about how when the Titanic actually went down, that men of noble birth and proper upbringing pushed aside the nuns and orphans to get their asses on the liferafts. Maybe that's the ugly side of evolution, the side you don't want to admit to, the side that knows that you'd do almost anything to save your own skins when the time came. The side that knows ties of friendship mean squat when your life is on the line and inaction means extinction. The fix had been in from the beginning with you as the bait and he bit, hard. The first spasm of being hooked jolted through his body.

Within the blink of an eye, you pull a hand free from the phony knot Dan had tied your hands with and slam it down on the phone's cradle to cut off the call. Rushing like a linebacker going for a sack, Dan tries to grab him by the arm and catches the mouthpiece of the phone across his forehead as Nikko brings it down in a desperate flailing arc. Before you can get up, he's pushed Dan aside onto the floor and makes a charge at Hale who is standing between him and the door.

It all seems like a slow motion playback as you try to lunge forward to grab him by the back of his pants. Since your feet are really tied, you aren't able to snap your arm out quick enough and end up missing entirely, your fingers glancing off of his jeans.

Originally, you think Hale intended to help Dan make the tackle on Nikko after the call was made. The problem was that after you had accidentally cracked his rib, he was in too much pain to think of much else. Consequently, when Nikko made a rush at him he was standing but not ready. Hale tries to bring the gun up into the charging face before him but is too slow. Nikko lowers his head and plows square into the middle of Hale's chest, sending him backwards in a howl of exploding pain. The gun flies out of his hands and Nikko rolls onto the ground on top of it.

You have just kicked your feet loose from the rope as he grabs the loose pistol. Like a cat he scoops it up and is back on his feet in a flash. Dan is slightly dazed and bleeding from the cut on his forehead as you leap off of the bed towards Nikko. In your mind's eye you see yourself on top of him before he has a chance to even see you. You had stolen ten bases last year and were pretty quick on a jump so you knew you could have him. Under normal circumstances, you would too.

Circulation has not yet returned to your feet and, as you hit the floor, your ankles buckle like saplings under the weight of your body. Before you can even realize it, you've fallen to your hands and knees as Nikko turns around with the gun in his hand.

As you rock back off of your hands, you are greeted by the unseeing black eye of a gun barrel winking back only an inch away from your face.

"I thought I was your friend, Scott?"

Is he shitting me? you think.

His grip stiffens on the handle and you watch as his whole body tenses up, waiting for the explosion from the muzzle as he pulls back on the trigger.

Click.

His eyes widen in disbelief as he pulls the trigger again three times more with the same result.

Click, click, click...

In the second you see him bring the gun back you know exactly what he is planning to do with it. Ignoring the throbbing of your ankles you jump to your feet and grab his arm before he can smash you in the face. Without a moment's hesitation, you ball up your fist and send it crashing into his face, flattening his nose like a squashed tomato. His head pitches backwards and you let him fall to the floor. To your surprise you realize you still have the strip of duct tape across your mouth. Grabbing at one of the corners you rip it off and throw it down.

"You want a friend?" you shout right in his ruined face. "Get a fucking dog!"

Within a second, Dan is on top of him making sure he isn't going to try something like that again. You had broken Nikko's nose good and he is barely able to even writhe in pain on the floor, let alone try to get away.

You dig the roll of duct tape out of his knapsack and bind his hands behind him and his feet together and toss him onto the bed. A little voice in your head is trying to tell you there isn't much time to spare. The police are going to show up any minute.

20

At first you think that Hale is hurt much worse than he actually is.

"How do you feel?"

"Like a hundred dollars." He forces a smile. You smile back at him weakly. It is going to be a long ride home. "Jeez, Scott, you didn't have to hit me that goddamned hard."

You are thinking the very same thing. Your jaw is still sore and you are pretty sure you are still bleeding too. You both know though it is completely necessary to make everything look right. Your ticker is running like a machine gun and you know the moment the adrenaline stops, the pain will flare up like a match on a bone dry haystack. The rush is back and is giving you the edge you need again to stay on your toes. This isn't over yet.

"Nothing personal," you say.

On the bed, Nikko's face is a runny mess from the crushed blob of flesh that used to be his nose. The sound of his breathing is weak and raspy through the river of blood and mucous.

"Do you think we'd give you a real gun you stupid lunatic?" Dan asks as he cinches the clothesline from Nikko's wrists to the bedframe.

You go over to the bed. Mr. P. is still there on the floor, all silent and purple. You try not to look at him but it is no use. Another innocent victim. You can't stop yourself from looking and wonder if this is all finally going to end here. As far as you are concerned, it does. Nikko stares pure hatred at you from the nether world of pain that he is in. You could care less.

After yesterday's incredible debacle it was clearly obvious what you were going to have to do with him. The way things were going, he'd never be able to stop. Each bomb was just going to lead to another bomb and another and another. It was a path of complete annihilation because sooner or later, he was going to get you all done for. The killing had to stop after today.

Hale and Dan came up with the plan last night after Nikko had left and, since you were asleep, you became the honeypot. You were the obvious choice because everything they had said about you was true. Chances are that right after Nikko, you were the one most likely to blow the house down and get everyone caught. In your state of semi-consciousness this morning before the two detectives showed up, you understood the basic idea behind the plan as Hale had laid it out. You knew there was no choice in the matter. You had to take Nikko out of the equation.

There was no doubt during the double-cross that you feared they really might kill you, that the scapegoat for the whole mess was really going to be you. You lean over Nikko, your friend. He would have sacrificed any of you in a heartbeat for his precious little bombs. There wasn't a person in this room that didn't know it either.

"You're the loose cannon, asshole," you tell him. "And a loose cannon will sink a whole goddamned ship if it isn't tied down or pushed overboard."

"Vug yew," he curses at you from behind his busted nose.

"Hey Scott, do you think we should put tape over his mouth?" asks Dan. "He can't breathe through his nose, it might suffocate him but I say let's do it anyway."

"Nah, don't bother," you tell him. "What are we, a bunch of animals? He'll get what's coming to him."

"Yeah, boom-boom fuckin' shithead," Dan says, leaning over Nikko.

You reach over to the TV and turn it up to full volume.

"Alright," Hale says, taking a deep breath, trying to regain his composure. "We're out of here."

"One last thing," you say.

You take a deep breath and jump into the bathroom quickly, shutting the door behind you. The timer hangs on the wall and you change the green *on* position from five o'clock to just a little past four. You dart back out the door and let out a great big sigh.

"We have just over ten minutes so I suggest we haul a little ass," you tell them. Something catches Hale's eye and he looks out the window.

"Oh man, the cops just showed up. We gotta hurry."

You open the door and make sure the hallway is clear. Dan and Hale go out first. You turn to Nikko one last time and throw him a mock salute.

"*Ad-yoze*, fuckhead."

He tries to say something back but you can't hear him over the television.

You rush down the hall, but something catches your eye. A security camera pointed right at you. You can't help it, you freeze. Hale grabs your arm and pulls you along. There is nothing you can do about it now.

By the elevator, Hale realizes with the cops in the parking lot already, you're going to need as much help getting out as possible so he reaches over to the fire alarm and pulls it. Instantly, the hallway fills with the loud clanging of a fire bell. You push the boys towards the fire door and scramble down the steps.

When you get to the ground floor, the scene is a total torrent of confusion and hysteria. Everyone inside the Grand Tropic is scrambling for the exits, and for a moment you are lost in a sea of people screaming and yelling for their friends and mothers and daughters and sisters and brothers and wives and husbands in a swarm of every language imaginable. The chaos is unbelievable. Dan pushes you behind a morbidly obese woman screaming hysterically who snowplows through the surging crowd. Using her as a blocking back, you push your way to the front door and are finally shoved outside by the screaming wave of people behind you.

As soon as you hit the sidewalk, you just keep going like

everyone else. Past the police who are trying to keep everyone calm, their cars pulling up out front with the lights still going. From far away you can hear the distant sirens of fire trucks and police cars headed in your direction. You tell the guys to just keep moving and not look back.

Checking your watch, you can see that it's just on top of four. You are half a block away and the curious rush past you to get closer, to get a better glimpse—to take pictures and video to show the poker buddies and co-workers and sewing circle back home. It is the truest form of human nature; it is life as show.

You fight your way to the end of the block and check the time again—three minutes after and still nothing. You break your no-look rule and cop a quick glance at the Grand Tropic. The cops are probably kicking in the door to 226 right now which means the three of you might just as well thumb your way to a firing squad. Maybe you forgot to close the bathroom door behind you and all of the gas just drifted away. Maybe Nikko got his dumb ass out of there somehow. Maybe you should just hail this cab coming down the street and get the hell out of Dodge and start thinking about Rio or Fiji or Africa. You tell the guys to wait up for a sec and raise your hand.

You're so close. You're going to make it. You think of the time in little league when you stole home. You think of Manny and those soft lips and long eyelashes.

The explosion hits just as the cab pulls up. It isn't big but it's big enough. At six minutes past four in the afternoon, room 226 and the empty room above it vaporize in a fireball that will only be attributed to the evils of neo-terrorism.

You stand there on the curb for a moment and watch the flames shoot from the windows of the hotel before getting into the cab. You let the guys pile into the back so Hale can have some room and you get up front next to the driver. You start to tell him where you're going but he is fixated on the burning hotel down the street.

"Holy Jeez, are they shooting a movie or something over there?"

"Yeah, that's what I heard," Dan replies. "Something called The Doomsday Squad or something like that, I think."

"Somebody said the Rock is in it," Hale adds.

"The Rock, huh? That guy ain't too bad. He ain't no Arnold though, right? Now that guy, he made some movies, boy." He puts the cab in drive and pulls away. "Where are you boys going again?"

"Bus station."

"Oh yeah. Hey, you guys see that Arnold movie with the alien?"

"Terminator."

"No."

"Predator."

"Yeah, that Arnold's one mean sumbitch, boy."

None of you even bother to look back at the hotel, you just talk action movies with the cabbie all the way to the Greyhound terminal. Well, those guys mostly talk. You chime in your two cents every now and then but mostly just stare out the window and watch the police cars, fire trucks and news-vans whiz past. Before you turn the corner you catch a glimpse of the Grand Tropic in the side-view mirror. What you've done is unspeakable.

You aren't in too much of a mood to bus it back to L.A. but the fake Florida driver's license you had gotten from the guy Snatch knew was in the men's room trashcan at the airport. If the police ever got around to checking records they'd find a Manny Hernandez who flew to Vegas today. You run a name like that in L.A. or Dade County and you'll get the phone book.

Just as you get to the bus station you watch the bus to L.A. pull away.

"Sorry boys, the next one's in an hour," the cabbie tells you.

You look at the guys and you check to see how much money you have between you. Much as you expect, Hale is loaded.

"Where's the next stop down the line?" you ask.

"A little town called Jean. It's about thirty-five miles down highway fifteen. Why?"

"Let's just say I have a pretty hot date that I'd really hate to miss," you tell him.

"Sorry, kid. It's too far off my beat," he tells you. "Can't take you there."

You look away and nod your head. It is what it is.

"You know kid, life is ten percent what you make it, and ninety percent how you take it."

It sinks in immediately like a downpour in the desert. At a crossroads where you are just starting to understand the tiniest bit about yourself, this is the signpost you had been looking for. The thing that gets you is that if none of this had ever happened, you never would have gotten the chance to see it.

"You know who said that?"

You shake your head. You just thought he had made it up on the spot.

"Irving Berlin," he tells you.

Irving Berlin? Is he kidding? The most profound thing you had ever heard in your sorry life came from the same place as "This is the Army Mr. Jones" and "White Christmas"? After all, a well is just another hole in the ground when you really think about it. Irving Berlin it is then. Maybe you've been listening to the wrong goddamned radio stations for years or something.

And when Hale taps you on the shoulder, you see the three black SUV's screech up, bubble lights flashing behind the windshield.

The cab screeches away. You look at each other. Your balls have gone into duck-and-cover mode as the Federal agents deploy, guns in motion being drawn down on you.

"Dan, no!" you try to yell, but he's already made a break for it.

It all seems like it's happening in slow motion. The first bullet hits him in the back. The next one catches him behind the ear. As he tumbles to the ground, Dan's body goes completely limp, falling like a lump of rags.

"Fucking bastards!" Hale screams. His hand reaches under his shirt and you grab his wrist as he pulls out the gun. Filling your ears is the sharp crack of gunfire as a jet of blood spurts from Hale's chest. He drops to his knees, then onto his back. The next slug catches you in the side in an explosion of pain that takes you off your feet. You fall next to Hale.

His breathing is quick and hitched. There is a whistle coming from his chest as the air from his lungs is pushed through the wound. He reaches over and grabs your hand and it feels cold to the touch.

"I'm going to miss the party..." you manage to say to him. You can feel consciousness slipping away from you. You can feel your blood ebbing from your body.

"You're gonna miss more than that," he weakly responds. You tell him to keep his strength. You tell him to hold on. He squeezes your hand.

In a whisper, Hale tells you when you got back to school, he was going to take Excalibur and his bong, drive down to Manhattan Beach Pier and throw them both into the ocean. You imagine riding down there with him. You imagine the sun setting over the Pacific. You imagine a nice breeze blowing through your hair, watching as they tumble end-over-end through the air into the sea and neither of you speaking another word about it to each other.

Also from GLENNEYRE PRESS...

THE ART OF SURFACING
by Mark Yoshimoto Nemcoff
isbn 0-9768040-9-3

The year is 1986, Ex-KGB agent Figen Dimyarian has come to Boston with British spies on his tail, a hundred million in stolen Russian funds, and enough insider information to turn a fortune on the American stock market. Burnt-out 28 year-old lawyer Alex Chase is pushing paper for his firm's largest client, EoGen Pharmaceuticals. Alex has discovered something is very wrong with Marpax, EoGen's next big drug, and the people who stand to profit from it want very much to keep it a secret. But who can he trust? Everyone at the firm seems out to get him, including Hope, a power hungry associate and Alex's former bedmate. When Alex learns that someone is killing off subjects in Marpax's FDA testing, and those people intend to murder Hope as well, he puts his life on the line for her. Alone and against all odds, he turns to the only one who can help—Figen, the same "imaginary friend" now on the run for his very own existence.

Available at AMAZON, BARNES&NOBLE.COM and wherever books are sold.

Log onto *www.glennneyrepress.com* now to find out more about our books including: THE ART OF SURFACING

About the Author

ALEX DAMIEN once pulled a knife on a drunk lawyer in Mexico to make the man stop punching his girlfriend in the face. The rest of that weekend, he claims, was fairly unremarkable. He currently lives in Los Angeles.

Printed in the United States
29745LVS00001B/457-489

9 780976 804000